Night work

Steve Higgs

To all the fans of funny thrillers.

Contents

1. Tears of an Ogre. East Kingsley, 1152hrs Friday, December 2nd   1

2. The Blue Moon Office. 1643hrs Friday, December 2nd   9

3. Swamp Monster? Friday, December 2nd 1737hrs   13

4. My Apartment, 0643hrs Saturday, December 3rd   20

5. Lunch. Saturday, December 3rd 1227hrs   40

6. Karen Gilbert's House. Saturday, December 3rd 1400hrs   45

7. Jennifer Lasseter. Saturday, December 3rd 1537hrs   53

8. Frank's Theories. Saturday, December 3rd 1624hrs   59

9. Self-defense. Saturday, December 3rd 1800hrs   65

10. My First Stakeout. Saturday, December 3rd 2018hrs   70

11. Fire. Sunday, December 4th 0048hrs   76

12. Tempest's House. Sunday, December 4th 0447hrs   84

13. Break ups. Sunday, December 4th 1303hrs   93

14. Fresh Evidence. Sunday December 4th 1512hrs   96

15. Maidstone Police Station. Sunday, December 4th 1530hrs   98

16. Biddenden Lake. Sunday, December 4th 1648hrs   103

17. Late Night Research. Sunday, December 4th 2246hrs   111

18. Cardiac Trauma. Monday, December 5th 0154hrs   118

19. Full Office. Monday, December 5th 0834hrs   119

20. Reformed Ogre. Monday, December 5th 0911hrs   127

21. Threats. Monday, December 5th 1022hrs   133

22. Pay Raise. Monday, December 5th 1039hrs   136

23. A Clue in a Puddle. Monday, December 5th 1547hrs   143

24. Swamp Monster. Monday, December 5th, no idea what time.   147

25. Familiar Territory. Monday, December 5th unsure of time   154

26. Sir Arthur. Monday, December 5th 2042hrs   158

27. Rescue. Monday, December 5th 2112hrs   164

28. Battle. Monday, December 5th 2149hrs   171

29. Mopping Up. Monday, December 5th 2254hrs   176

30. Epilogue   181

31. What's next for the Blue Moon gang?   184

32. Lord Hale's Monster   185

33. More Books by Steve Higgs   186

About the Author   187

Tears of an Ogre. East Kingsley, 1152hrs Friday, December 2nd

I ARRIVED AT THE entrance to Queen's park in East Kingsley going too fast. My little Ford Fiesta wasn't built for speed and most certainly not for cornering hard which I found out to my dismay as I threw it into a hard, right turn and felt the back end drifting out. The speed was a result of the ticking clock. The ticking clock because I doubted I had much time left and still had some distance to cover on foot.

The drive from the office in Rochester High Street, where I had been, to the park in West Kingsley ought to take twenty minutes. Traffic had been light though as schools and offices were still operating but I had to stop to pick something up en route; something I knew I would need, so the journey took me almost half an hour despite the empty road and my heavy foot.

Had another car been coming out of the park, I would have caused a crash. Thankfully, there wasn't, so I swung the car wide, the rear end skidding sideways a bit on the fallen leaves, until I righted it once more and sprang forward. With my heart thumping from almost killing myself, I slowed to a more survivable speed as I reached the brow of the small slope that led into the car park.

Today my name is Jane Butterworth and I work at the Blue Moon Investigation Agency, a firm that specializes in cases with a paranormal or just plain strange element. Tempest Michaels opened the business just a few months back in the Spring of this year, but demand for his services resulted in fast growth and he took on a new investigator in the form of ex-cop Amanda Harper and then me as an admin assistant. Somehow my role has morphed into something more than admin though.

I say it happened somehow, but the truth is that it happened because I thought it might be fun to try solving a case by myself. The case in question was to do with a vampire, or, at least, sort of to do with a vampire.

Not so very long ago at all, I was still living in the closet and allowing my suppressed side to voice itself by being part of a vampire Live Action Role Play or LARP club. LARP allowed me to dress up and do fun stuff. And it was through the club that I met Tempest, when my grandmother, who I lived with at the time, called him because she thought I might bite her neck one night. The club broke up and, a little lost, I finally admitted to myself that I was gay and that I liked wearing girl clothes. Almost overnight, my female personality, Jane, was born.

I now have two personalities. Not like a schizophrenic, but like a person that is truly gender neutral and lets mood determine which underwear drawer I pick from each morning. Somedays I am James and I dress to the left. Other days I am Jane and do my best to pretend I don't have a penis.

As I pulled into the carpark, I saw the park warden standing in plain sight. He was waiting for me and recognized the car or perhaps me behind the wheel. Whatever the case, he certainly knew it was me and was waving for me to hurry before I could even get the handbrake on.

'Don't worry about paying for parking,' he called. 'I'll put a sign on it in case the local council parking officer turns up.'

'Where is he?' I asked.

'The parking officer?'

I shook my head like he was being dumb; the adrenalin making me bouncy and over-excited. 'No, the ogre.'

'Oh. Yeah, that should have been obvious. In his usual place. Just scared a load of mums who were out with their babies. This is really not cool, you know. I called again, like you asked, but this has to be the last time, Jane.'

'Yeah, I got it.' I took off running, not that I could go very fast. I had on killer high heels today and they were designed for being tall in, not moving at speed.

The park warden wasn't done though. As I ran across the grass toward the bridge, he shouted, 'Last time, Jane. You tell him that. Next time I will call the police myself.' I didn't turn or bother answering; nothing could be gained by it.

Queen's Park in West Kingsley is a wide expanse of trees and fields running alongside a river. It has several bridges that cross over it where kids go to play Pooh sticks or feed the ducks. It was a place where local people walked their dogs or went for some open-air fitness. Families took picnics there on a warm day and like most parks, it was a lovely place to go.

Recently though it had developed a new attraction: an ogre. He jumped out from beneath the bridge and generally scared the crap out of anyone passing by. The park warden had first called Tempest almost a month ago after reports of a giant ugly creature living beneath one of the three bridges in the park could no longer be ignored. At that time, the reports were from school children on their way home and a few old ladies walking their pugs and poodles or early morning joggers getting the surprise of their lives as the disgusting swamp creature jumped out and screamed for them to get off his bridge.

In typical Tempest style, he had staked out the park, lying in wait in a shallow trench he dug for himself in the middle of the night. When the sun began to come up, he saw the ogre climb down from the path and position itself beneath the bridge. He waited then until he could catch the creature in the act and sprang from his hiding place as a jogger came down the path and the ogre got ready to jump out.

Tempest issued a loud verbal warning but unheeded, the ogre proceeded to scare the heck out of the poor chap running down the path with his head-phones on. So, Tempest tackled him, performing a move he calls the reverse leg sweep. I don't know what that is, but it had no effect other than to enrage the ogre who picked him up and threw him in the river. Tempest had responded with an intent to do whatever violence was necessary to subdue the fellow but before the first punch was thrown, the ogre held up his hands in surrender.

It wasn't an ogre, of course. It was just a man, but in this case, a homeless man who probably had some mental health issues. The park and indeed the bridge were famous as the subject of a book written many years ago. *The Ogre under the Bridge* was a childhood classic story of a little boy who grew up alone in a big house and had no friends because his father was the local rich person. When he found an ogre living under the bridge in the park near his house, the two of them set off on quests together. I remembered my grandmother reading me the book when I was little.

The giant man Tempest faced, seemed confused about what he might have done wrong; his attempts to scare people were intended only to give them an exciting experience and remind them of the joyous children's tale.

Arthur wore tatty clothes and had an unkempt beard and hair. He stood around seven feet tall and was perfect for playing the part of an ogre. Assuming he was homeless, Tempest offered him a hot meal and walked him out of the park and into the small town of West Kingsley where, over hot bacon rolls, Arthur agreed to give up his role as the ogre. That appeared to be that, and Tempest closed the case.

Tempest had thought it settled but a few days later, the park warden called again: Arthur was back. Whether from boredom or lack of memory, he had gone back to hiding under the bridge and jumping out to scare people again.

Tempest dealt with it again. And again two days later. It would have been simple enough to get the police involved but Tempest didn't want that. In his conversations with Arthur, he learned that the man's wife had died two years ago and, all alone, he had regressed to a childlike outlook on life. He kept using the word quest and insisting he be referred to as Sir Arthur. After the fourth incident, it had gone quiet but when Tempest went to France to deal with the Yeti, he asked me to give my number to the wardens in case Arthur did it again. Which he did, about an hour after Tempest left. I didn't bother to tell him or Amanda about it, I just got in my car and dealt with it.

He promised he wouldn't do it again, but it was clear to me that whatever had driven him to act out the part of ogre under the bridge the first time, now he was doing it because it was fun: I doubted he had many friends.

He had been hungry at the time. It was a cold November day, so, remembering Tempest's tactic, I got him away from the bridge by enticement in the form of a hot sandwich in a local café. We must have looked quite the sight; a petite blond woman and a seven-foot monster with bits of tree in his hair. They let us in though from the look I got, I was fairly certain they wouldn't do so again.

That brought me back to today and the latest call from the angry park warden. Having crossed the field diagonally, the fastest way to get to the bridge from the car park, I grimaced at the state of my beautiful heels. They were covered in mud and I had marks on my stockings. Mumbling to myself that Arthur needed to hope they would clean up, I heard the distant wail of a cop car's siren: the mums had called the police no doubt. Fearing I had no time to lose, I approached the bridge making plenty of noise to attract his attention.

Sure enough, the great lummox leapt out to scare me, making horrendous growling screeching noises which ended when he started to say, 'Get off my bridge!'

Feeling distinctly like kicking him in the nuts, I said, 'Again?' filling my question with a heavy dose of dismay and disappointment. It shut him up instantly. 'You promised me you wouldn't do this again, I pointed out. The police are coming you know?'

'Sorry, Miss Jane,' he said, his head bowed in shame.

I sighed. He was huge and scary and menacing, but he was also a bit pathetic, so I had to remind myself I was basically dealing with a homeless man who most likely had a limited IQ. 'I brought you a sandwich,' I said, producing the double-wrapped toasted BLT I stopped for en route.

His head came up and his eye sparkled. 'For me?'

'Yes, but only if you come with me. You can't stay here, and you can't come back here. Jumping out and scaring people isn't funny.'

'It's not supposed to be funny,' he complained. 'It is the start of a great adventure. I am inspiring kids and adults alike to find their own quests and reminding them of how special this place is. It inspired a story that dominated my life, you know?'

'Yes, I know Arthur. Now come on, we have to get moving.' When he didn't shift, I shouted. 'Now, Arthur!' and stamped my foot which snapped the heel of my shoe clean off. I said some choice words at that point and balanced on one foot while I stared disbelievingly at my favourite footwear. Seeing my rage, Arthur tried to get back below the bridge. 'Hey, Arthur. Get back out here. What would your mother think?'

The words just came to me. I couldn't tell you why I thought bringing his mother into it might work, but it did. 'Mummy?' he echoed. 'Mummy would be cross. Mummy said I had to be nice.'

'Yes, well, this isn't nice, Arthur. You are being bad, and you need to stop.'

'Because that is what mummy would want?'

'Yes,' I replied, making myself sound confident but really not sure how he would now react. Whatever I had expected, it wasn't tears. His face crumpled, and salty drops were running off his scraggly beard as he began to bawl.

The sirens, which had been getting louder and closer suddenly shut off; the cops were here. They would still have to cross the field, but they wouldn't be doing it in high heels. I grabbed Arthur's arm, kind of hopping and limping with my shoe back on my foot but the heel in my handbag.

'Come on, Arthur. You can still make your mum proud, but we must get going. Right now,' I added when he didn't move. He still didn't move; he just tipped his head back and howled his unhappiness. I tugged his arm, but I might as well have been trying to move the bridge for all the impact I had. Arthur had to weigh two-hundred pounds more than me and I could hear voices now; the cops shouting instructions to each other.

If we didn't move soon, we were going to be in big trouble. Not just him, me too probably given how often Tempest got arrested. 'Hey, Arthur. If you come with me now, I'll get you some cake to go with the sandwich. How does that sound?'

'Cake?' he asked, the tears switching off as suddenly as they started.

'Yes, cake.' I gave his arm another tug, this time managing to make him trudge along with me as we crossed the bridge that would lead us out of the park and into the village. 'We need to hurry though.' I tried to explain.

Clearly my urgency had some resonance because I was suddenly and unexpectedly scooped into the air as he picked me up like a baby and began running. I started to demand that he put me down, but I stopped myself as I saw how fast we were now moving. The shouts of the unseen uniformed officers faded behind us as he followed the twisting path through the woods. I had to crane my neck to see where we were going but could see the woods thinning ahead of us.

I patted his arm to get his attention. 'Put me down now, we are coming to the road.'

He complied just as we reached the end of the path and shimmied through the barriers designed to keep bikes out. I didn't know if we were safe or not and I was now more than a mile from my car, which I would have to return to.

My companion had other concerns though. 'Cake?' he prompted.

'Yes, Arthur. Now it's time for cake. Well done, by the way. That was some very impressive running then.'

'Sandwich?' he prompted, lest I forget that I had a sandwich for him in my bag. Still hobbling along in my broken shoe, I fished in the bag to retrieve his meal, happy to have it out of my bag where the bacon was bound to leave a scent for days to come. Just what every girl wants: the smell of bacon following her around. It would make me popular with dogs if nothing else.

Arthur opened the foil wrapping with one meaty fist and performed a disappearing trick on the sandwich; in four bites the whole thing was gone, and his still-hungry expression reminded me of a dog that wants a treat one second after it has swallowed the previous one as if the memory bank is wiped clean each time.

Thankfully, the remaining distance to the coffee shop in town took only a few minutes and Arthur gave me his arm to make walking easier. Next to the coffee shop was one of those shops that cuts keys, and sells trophies, and puts heels back on shoes. The chap behind the counter scratched his head and said, 'I'll give it a go.' So, then barefoot, I took Arthur for cake.

The Blue Moon Office. 1643hrs Friday, December 2nd

A little more than four hours later, I was winding down for the day and getting ready to go home. I would be knocking off a few minutes early, but I was okay with that and I knew Tempest would be okay with it too. I regularly worked extra hours, answered calls from either Tempest or Amanda on days off or during the evening and stayed late whenever it felt necessary. I didn't complain about doing it and Tempest was always grateful for my efforts. The Blue Moon Investigation Agency was just the kind of business where normal office hours didn't really apply.

The two investigators, Tempest and Amanda, solved a lot of cases at night. I can't say if the same is true for other detective agencies but at Blue Moon it was fairly standard simply because of the weird nature of the cases – you don't get vampires, werewolves or ghosts during the day.

Anyway, after my hurried run through West Kinglsey park to get to Arthur, my feet were sore. The cobbler managed to fix my heel though he warned it would never be as strong as it was when new, so my feet looked great but were ready to be set free and stuffed into a pair of fluffy slippers instead. Collecting my phone, lipstick and nail file from the desk, I put them in my handbag as I took my keys out. The unicorn keyring I kept them on had seen better days; the fluffy white mane was no longer white and the fuzz on the pink horn had worn through to show the plastic beneath but I twirled it on my finger as I switched off my desk lamp and shut down the computer.

I was less than a second from walking to the back door when the phone rang. My right foot twitched to walk away, but I sighed instead, put my handbag back down and snatched up the desk phone. 'Blue Moon Investigations, Jane speaking. How may I help you?'

'Good evening, this is PC Van Doorn of Kent police. Can I speak with Tempest Michaels please?'

I leaned across the desk to grab a pad and pen. Normally when I answer the phone, I find it easier to create a note on the computer, but it was off so pen and paper would have to do as if I were a luddite caveperson. Cradling the handset under my chin while I worked the pen to write down the caller's name was awkward, so I flicked it onto speaker. 'Hello, PC Van Doorn. I'm afraid Tempest is temporarily unavailable. We have other investigators here though. What is the nature of your business?' As I asked the question, I realised the constable probably wasn't calling to report a paranormal anomaly he wanted us to investigate. More likely it was something else or he would have announced himself by name, not rank.

'I am under instruction that it has to be Tempest Michaels. Under no circum-stances can it be Amanda Harper, Miss Butterworth.' He knew my last name without me saying it, so the boy had done some homework. Of course, one could find such information on our website easily enough. I had a great picture on the website because I constructed and ran it. Whether to go with a boy picture or a girl picture had been a question I debated for almost a week at the time, but in the end, I simply selected the best picture I had. It just happened to be one where I wore my blonde wig and made sure my adams apple wasn't visible.

I was curious now though. Why was he insisting that Amanda couldn't be the investigator? 'Can you tell me why, please?'

'Why what?'

'Why it must not be Miss Harper,' I demanded.

He dropped his voice to a hushed whisper when he answered, 'It's something to do with Chief Inspector Quinn. I'm calling on his behalf. He wants to hire Tempest Michaels and was most clear that he would kill me if Amanda Harper turned up.'

Ah. That explained it. I wasn't sure what the history was between Amanda and her old chief inspector, but she hated him, and he seemed to loathe her. His request for Tempest's help was a new thing though. I said, 'Very good,' because I couldn't think of anything else to say, then decided to start lying my arse off. 'Actually, Miss Harper is not available either, but the initial investigation and research is always conducted by me so the best person to attend a meeting and get the ball going is me.' There wasn't much truth in that statement. Yes, I did the research, but mostly that was on Tempest's instruction. I had recently taken on a case of my own though that Tempest didn't know about yet. Buoyed by solving that by myself, I believed I could get this case started for him. He had been away a few days already so was bound to be back soon. When he returned, I would present him with a case file and research ready to go.

That ought to win a few points.

'Can I ask the nature of the case?'

'The chief inspector does not wish the details discussed over the phone. He said that Mr Michaels would be interested enough to attend and he would tell him then.'

'Well, it will be me for the first meeting or no one, I'm afraid. What time in the morning would be convenient?'

'Oh, um. Actually, I believe he expected Mr Michaels to come directly.'

Oh, did he?

I didn't know the chief inspector, but I had heard Tempest talking about him using some rather colourful and descriptive language. Tempest didn't swear much so it stuck out when he did. I gave another sigh and accepted that I was going. I got a huge buzz from solving the last case, and ever since had been toying with the idea that I might approach Tempest about taking on another one. With both he and Amanda out of the country, I could legitimately take this on and see how it went.

Getting ready to end the call, I said, 'Please tell the chief inspector I will be there in thirty minutes.' PC Van Doorn thanked me and advised that I should ask for him at the front desk when I arrived.

With the call done, I cleared my throat. I had been doing girl voice more and more recently and though I felt I was getting better at it, it made my throat hurt after a while. I spoke in my normal baritone just to ease the dull ache and drank the last of the water in the glass on my desk. Suddenly wondering what I was getting into and then wondering why I had thought this was a good idea, I grabbed my bag once more and headed to the car park.

Swamp Monster?
Friday, December 2nd
1737hrs

AT A LITTLE AFTER five o'clock on a Friday, traffic through the Medway towns was murder. Offices had kicked out and the old narrow streets couldn't handle the converging traffic. My normal route home didn't take me through the towns but around them, driving almost twice the distance but in half the time. But, bumper to bumper for thirty-five minutes and I arrived at the police station in Maidstone a few minutes later than predicted.

The desk sergeant stood up as I approached, glaring at me from behind the counter. In front of him was a young female police officer, her brown hair cut into a tidy bob. She flicked her eyebrows at me in greeting. 'Good evening.'

'Hi, Jane Butterworth to see Chief Inspector Quinn. I was instructed to ask for PC Van Doorn.'

'Yes, take a seat, please,' she said while indicating the row of plastic chairs behind me. 'Someone will be out to collect you shortly.'

'Are there restrooms?' I asked looking about. The water I drank at the office had filtered through me on the journey over and I was about to go into a meeting.

'Just along the corridor,' the female PC indicated, this time to the left. Following her hand, I saw the sign for the ladies and set off.

As I reached the door, I heard the sergeant speak for the first time. 'Excuse me. Where do you think you're going?'

I was halfway through the door of the ladies but froze, rooted to the spot and embarrassed even before I turned around to face him. His younger female colleague was staring at him with a confused face. 'She asked where the toilets were,' she explained as if he were being ridiculous.

He had a cruel smile on his lips though. 'You're Tempest Michaels's freak, aren't you? I heard about you. I must say when they told me you actually look like a girl, I figured they were exaggerating. You'll use the gents toilet though. Thank you very much.' When I didn't move, he frowned at me. 'Go on now, James. There's a good boy.'

Mortified, but seeing no course of action that would save me face, I complied, letting the door to the ladies toilet go as I trudged to the mens' bog instead. I didn't meet many people that were truly bothered by my choice to cross-dress, but those that did always seemed to be in a position of power and thus had the ability to be as awful as they liked.

When I returned to the plastic chairs a minute later, the girl at the desk made a silent apology with her eyes but the sergeant didn't even bother to look up. I held my head high and refused to let my cheeks colour as I walked in front of him. I didn't make it to the seat though. A cheerful voice attached to a cheerful face got my attention instead as a door opened next to the counter.

'Miss Butterworth?' the cheerful face said as he stuck out his hand to shake. 'PC Van Doorn. Are you ready?' I was still smarting from being called out a moment ago and knew that I wouldn't tolerate it if the chief inspector was equally horrible. PC Van Dorn was a delight though. He shot me a big smile as he held the door and, my goodness, he was nice to look at. Six feet three inches tall, or maybe a little more, deep blue eyes I just wanted to swim in and a pretty, pretty face. I was in a serious relationship and lived with a guy, but it didn't hurt to look, right? Plus, Simon had been a bit of a dick when I called him from the car to say I would be late home this evening. He wanted dinner and didn't like that I had a job. He had more than enough money for both of us and made it clear he would much rather I stayed at home to look after his needs. Well, stuff that. I would take it up with him later and no doubt he would apologise and that would lead to some fooling around.

That was for later though. Right now I was pursuing a case and trying not to stare at PC Van Doorn's muscular bottom as I followed him through the station. He led me along a corridor, around a corner and up some stairs. At the top, the stairs opened out into an open-plan office which bustled with activity. Almost, but not quite everyone was in uniform and those that were not were wearing suits with ties as if that were the only alternative attire. Perhaps it was.

On the far side of the room were more offices, and as we approached, I saw a man I recognised as Chief Inspector Quinn. He looked to be somewhere around forty years old and about six feet tall. He had the body of an endurance athlete, which is to say that he looked fit, but from running not lifting weights like Tempest. He had a female police officer in his office with him, receiving instructions by the look of it.

PC Van Doorn paused at the door while he knocked and waited to be called to enter. The female officer left, exchanging the briefest of glances with me as she came through the door. Then PC Van Doorn caught it before it could close and held it for me to go in. Only once I was in the room did the chief inspector look up from the paperwork on his desk.

'Oh,' he said, expecting Tempest and getting me instead. 'I expected Mr Michaels.'

I jumped in quickly. 'Yes, he is temporarily unavailable but didn't want to make you wait. I'm his assistant Jane Butterworth.'

'Yes, I know who you are,' he replied. He said the words as if he had something else to say about me, but he didn't follow up.

'With his growing caseload, I often perform the initial research to get things moving,' I explained, hoping my slow drive over hadn't been a waste of time. To press the matter forward, I lifted the flap on my handbag, took out a small tablet to record notes and sat, unbidden, in the chair on my side of his desk. It felt like something Tempest would do; taking control of the situation to achieve the outcome he wanted. 'How can Blue Moon be of assistance, sir?'

The chief inspector looked like he was going to ask me to leave, but looking directly at me with an unreadable expression when he opened his mouth to speak, he said, 'Close the door, please, Van Doorn.' Then, as I poised my fingers for taking notes, he pushed some paperwork across the desk. 'You'll need to sign this non-disclosure agreement first, Miss Butterworth.' Then he waited patiently while I scanned it, added my signature and handed it back. Leaning back in his chair, he asked a question. 'Are you familiar with the swamp monster murder?'

Suddenly feeling like a kid in school that hasn't been paying attention, I said, 'No.'

He inclined his head in a gesture that I read as not surprised, then he started talking, 'It was three years ago now. A man drowned in Biddenden Lake. He was camping with his girlfriend in a remote spot and was found by her in the morning, floating near the edge of the lake. Her report was that she saw a creature in the water when she approached him. She was adamant about it, refusing to change her story throughout the investigation. She even had a drawing produced of the creature she described. Someone, we never found out who, leaked the picture to the press which resulted in the case being sensationalized and the ridiculous swamp monster name.'

'The girlfriend, Jennifer Lasseter, was the prime suspect. By her own admission there was no one else around and the only shoe prints at the scene were hers and his. I was the lead investigator at the time, it was my first case as a chief inspector and the national news interest meant a lot of senior eyes were on me from the start. There were no leads though and the victim was a large man; a body builder and he was not only twice as heavy as the suspect but far stronger. Her lawyer quickly argued that she could not have overpowered him and there were no signs of injury on her that she would surely have sustained. Furthermore, he produced evidence that Jennifer Lasseter could not swim and had a recorded fear of open bodies of water. I had never heard of such a thing but I soon discovered it is common enough to have a name: thalassophobia. The victim's body looked like it had been in a fight and the postmortem bruising produced web-shaped handprints. Not only that, there were bite marks on him, some of which had bitten chunks of flesh right off his bones. The species of creature blamed for the attack could not be identified, the forensic pathologists were stumped, and I had no case and no choice but to let the suspect go.' He fell silent for a while, staring into nothing as he ordered his thoughts. The silence stretched out long enough that I began to feel uncomfortable and wondered if I should say something. 'To this day, it is the only case I haven't solved,' he said, finally.

'How can we help?' I asked again, admittedly enthralled by the story, but unsure what it was that he wanted us to do with a three-year-old cold case.

The chief inspector brought his focus back to me. 'In the last three weeks there have been two more unexplained drownings at the lake. Both were men and both were police officers involved in the swamp monster case and the investigation afterwards. Their bodies were found by campers in both instances, both have postmortem bruising with webbed handprints and the same bite marks with missing bits of flesh. So far as I can make out, there is no motive, no suspect and I have no leads. I cannot even establish what the men might have been doing at the lake. Neither one was an angler or avid camper which might have placed them there deliberately. So, what do I want from Tempest Michaels? He specializes in weird. This is weird. I have a fund which can be used to employ specialist consultants so I want him to help me solve this case.' With the final line delivered, he pushed back into his chair and looked away. He seemed annoyed by the situation, or maybe it was asking for help that upset him. Whatever it was, he had an unexplained case and he wanted us to take it.

I felt jubilant. 'Is there a casefile?' I asked.

'PC Van Doorn will provide you with a copy of the original casefile and all the notes I have since the first new death three weeks ago. Van Doorn,' he called to get the younger man's attention.

'Yes, sir?'

'You will act as liaison to Miss Butterworth and Mr Michaels. Make sure she has contact details for you.'

'Yes, sir.' And just like that, the chief inspector went back to his papers. He didn't offer to shake my hand or even wish me luck. It was as if he had already forgotten I was there. Sensing that I had been dismissed, I tucked my tablet away and got up to leave. What would Tempest have done at this point? Probably knocked the man's coffee over to make a point about manners, but as I stood, the chief inspector had one more thing to say. 'You will remember to keep Miss Harper away from this case, won't you? I won't tolerate her incompetence.'

I wasn't sure if he expected an answer or not, but I gave one automatically. 'I understand.' It was all I could think of to say because I wanted to argue that I thought her to be brilliant but saw no benefit to be gained from doing so. PC Van Doorn closed the door behind me, and I was done.

'I'll get you that case file,' he said, walking fast to get around me as I made my way back to the stairs. 'I'll need to copy it first though.'

'What? Hold on. You mean it is a paper file?' I asked, my tone incredulous.

He laughed. 'Yes, we still have physical files here. A lot of it is kept electronically, but physical files, with handwritten paper reports and actual prints of photographs are still used. We gather all manner of physical evidence which cannot be stored electronically so...' I gave him a single eyebrow rise to show my feelings on the matter. He laughed again but we were back at the reception desk already. 'I'll bring it to the office in the morning, shall I?'

'You know where it is?'

'I have the address. I'm sure I'll find it,' he replied, still smiling.

I checked my watch to find it was almost six thirty. This had taken longer than I estimated. 'I have to get going, I'll see you tomorrow.' Like a gentleman, he zipped around me to open the front door. A blast of cold air hit me, making the skin on my neck goosepimple. I suppressed a shudder and pulled my coat tight.

As I walked the few steps down from the station to the pavement, I grimaced to myself about the conversation I most likely had waiting for me at home. Simon had been surly earlier, a behavioural trait most usually brought on by a bad day at the office. That I was unexpectedly late getting home and dinner was thus delayed wouldn't help. Thinking about Simon made me think about PC Van

Doorn though and how nice he had been. However, as I fished around for my car keys, I told myself that he was being nice because I was dressed and acting like a pretty blonde woman and he was doing what most young men would do in such circumstances.

Better for me that he was pleasant to spend time with though, if I was going to have a crack at this case. I would do some research into the swamp monster before bed.

Then a thought occurred to me.

My Apartment,
0643hrs Saturday,
December 3rd

THE THOUGHT I HAD thought kept me awake half the night. More so than the fight with Simon did anyway. Simon was calm when I got home, even apologizing for being short with me on the phone. But his attitude soon shifted when I told him I would be working over the weekend and couldn't predict how many hours I would be putting in.

The more I thought about it, the more I wanted to be an investigator like Tempest and Amanda. I was a little worried about how often the two of them seemed to get into fights or scrapes of some kind, but I would just have to toughen up. Maybe I would take a fight class like Tempest and Big Ben.

Anyway, Simon had come close to ranting at one point. He planned for us to visit friends and have lunch out while doing some shopping; Simon's favourite activity. That his hobby was buying things had always worked out well for me, but it wasn't much of a hobby in my opinion; I wanted something more exciting to do. It was one of the reasons the vampire LARP club enticed me: I got to dress up and pretend to be someone else and... well, it's behind me now, but Simon insisted I call the police and tell them I wasn't available until Monday when normal office hours resumed.

I refused, of course, and he slept with his back to me as I sat in bed with my laptop. Going back to the thought that kept me awake; it was about a Yeti. I hadn't heard from Tempest since early on Friday morning when he needed more research; this time on plastic surgery in Paris. He was getting close to cracking the case it seemed so not hearing from him either meant he was dead, or they had caught the bad guys and were celebrating. I emailed him but got no reply, which again, was unusual.

Tempest always sent me a text or email to say a particular case was closed so I could record it for billing purposes. Then I remembered Amanda. She had gone out there to join him and I had only one reason why she would do that: they were hooking up. I saw how they looked at each other so maybe they finally worked it out and were even now, rolling around in bed together.

It was that or he really was dead; he took such incredible risks sometimes. That was my last thought as I finally fell asleep and my first thought when I woke up. I fished for my phone on the bedside table, but my arm was the wrong way up as I lay in bed, so I had to sit up a bit to spot where it was. There, on the screen, was a message from Tempest answering my email from last night.

I read his message with my jaw hanging open. We deal with weird all the time, but this was right up there on the unbelievable scale. The Yeti was a surgically altered polar bear and the client's daughter, the one that was supposed to be dead, was behind it all.

The clock on my phone told me it wasn't even seven yet. Our usual Saturday routine involved sex and a lie in and watching TV with cups of tea sometimes followed by sex again. We hadn't been together all that long, a few months really, so the shine of the new relationship and the newness of exploring each other was still there.

Except it wasn't. Not this morning anyway. Even if he had gotten over himself in the night, I was feeling disinterested and I had purpose to my day. I slipped silently from the covers and went for a shower.

Having two personalities, one male, one female, meant I had a larger wardrobe than most people. I actually felt like being James today, but all my boy clothes were in the bedroom with Simon and my Jane wardrobe was in the spare room so that was where I got dressed.

A couple of weeks ago, I went undercover for Amanda as a date for a suspect and needed to look more convincingly female so had worn a fake bra. It was supposed to be a one-time thing, but I liked how it filled the loose material in the front of my dresses so now I wore it whenever I was Jane. Wearing that, a satin camisole and matching French knickers, I selected a white cotton blouse with thin pink pinstripes and a grey skirt suit. Delicate heels would work best with the outfit, but I could see the clouds outside despite the darkness, so I went with knee-high black leather boots, the ones with the chunky heel. They would be both safer to walk in and keep my legs warmer.

After toast and eggs for breakfast, I left Simon a note expressing that I was excited about what was happening with my career and hoped we could talk about it tonight over a bottle of wine. He mostly scoffed at my job, not in a scathing way, but he didn't see how it could develop into something more worthwhile than the admin role I currently held, and said as much last night. Maybe he would be proven right. Maybe I would stuff up this investigation and make the firm look bad. But maybe I wouldn't and last night, while doing some research into the first murder three years ago, I decided I was going to find out.

It was just after eight thirty when I parked my car in its usual spot behind the office. I didn't go in straight away though. I left the house before Simon got up and made as little noise as possible so I wouldn't wake him. Doing that though meant I didn't get a decent cup of coffee, just the instant stuff, and I wasn't going to wait for the fandango machine in the office to warm up. Instead, I walked to the coffee shop across the High Street.

Rochester High Street is a delightful place, filled with little eateries and completely devoid of franchise chains. One could find rare first edition books in quaint little shops or Victorian sweets in Ye Olde Sweete Shoppe. It was a tourist area with the castle, cathedral, and one-time house of Charles Dickens, and the architecture was incredible. The buildings in the pedestrianized High Street were hundreds of years old but all in fine condition and supported by funding to keep them that way. Of course, the tiny alleyways and dark shadows were also home to cutthroats and thieves so murder and other crimes would and did occur when the sun set.

Right now though, even though it was still dark, the early morning sun was beginning to chase away the black of night and I could see it glinting off the fancy weather vanes high above me.

A bell tinkled above my head as I pushed the coffee shop door open and went inside. The scent of fresh coffee hit me instantly but mixed in with it I could discern the smell of warm toast and sweet pastries. My stomach gave a growl as it placed its vote.

At the counter was a brunette woman. 'Good morning, Jane. What'll it be this morning?'

The badge pinned to the top of her apron gave the world her name, but I already knew it. 'Hi, Hayley. I'll take a tall americano and a cinnamon bun, please.'

'Nothing for Tempest?' she asked. I had the sense that she and Tempest had a little history. I didn't know what it was, and I wasn't going to ask, but she always found a reason to ask me about him.

'He's away,' I replied, handing over my card to pay. If she was disappointed, she masked it well, dismissing me with a smile as she moved to the next customer. Standing at the end of the counter while one of her colleagues made my drink and brought my pastry, I checked my phone and wondered if I should send Simon a message. I could easily convince myself I was in love with him, but we had been a little shaky recently; I wanted to get back to how we were.

I couldn't think what to write though, so I put my phone away as the drink and little bag arrived, thanked the server and went back out through the door as a pair of workmen held it open for me. I could feel them staring at my bum as I crossed the street, the tinkling of the bell absent behind me as they were still standing in the doorway and probably nudging each other.

Lights blinked into life as I settled at my desk and put my coffee down. The office was a large rectangular space with two separate offices at the back. Tempest and Amanda took one each, using them for private meetings when clients came to the office. Often as not their offices were empty and client meetings were conducted at the client's house or place of work.

My desk was set up in the main office. There wasn't room for it anywhere else and it doubled as reception for anyone that chose to visit us. My first task this morning was to put more time into researching the drowning three years ago. PC Van Doorn was bringing me the file, which would contain interview information and other details I wouldn't be able to find online. Last night, while distracted by worry over Tempest's silence and filled with concern over my fight with Simon, I had found newspaper articles from the original case. Such things were simple to find online, but right there had been the drawing of the swamp monster. It looked ridiculous; a mishmash of different parts or monster clichés all thrown together. It had a lizard face and spines running down its back. It could have been Godzilla from an early movie and for all I knew, it was.

As I booted my computer to life, a voice disturbed my train of thought. 'Hello.'

I looked up to see a nervous-looking woman standing just inside the doorway. I hadn't heard her come in, not that we had a bell like the coffee shop, but she seemed rooted to the spot with indecision.

I fixed a welcoming smile to my face and took a mental second to make sure my vocal cords were set to girl voice; I didn't want to startle the poor woman. 'Good morning, how can I help you?' Sometimes we got people that wandered in thinking the business was a recruitment agency or a stationer despite the sign outside that clearly stated Blue Moon Investigation Agency. This wasn't such a case though, the lady had apparently deliberately sought us out, and had just been lucky that I had come in on a Saturday.

'I'm, ah. I'm not sure,' she stuttered. The woman was somewhere in her early thirties with dark brown shoulder length hair. It had a natural curl that threatened unruliness but was tamed with clips and pulled into a ponytail behind her head. Her eyes peered out from round, wide-rimmed glasses and she wore little make up, perhaps a swipe of mascara only. Her outfit was jeans, ankle boots and a Hermes jacket, expensive and tasteful. All this I took in and considered in the first second. She looked about ready to bolt but she also looked like she had a genuine problem to discuss. Tempest would offer her a drink and a soothing tone, so that was what I did, teasing her toward the couches next to the expensive coffee machine.

Her feet moved reluctantly, but she sat when I suggested she make herself comfortable and I took a moment to turn on the coffee machine before I sat opposite her. 'I'm Jane,' I introduced myself. 'If I can help you, I will. The Blue Moon Investigations Agency specialises in... unusual cases. While the machine warms up would you like to tell me what brings you here today?' When she hesitated, I added, 'I can assure you complete confidentiality.'

The lady hung her head as if ashamed for what she was about to reveal but then brought it up again to meet my eyes. 'I am having vivid dreams that I don't think are actually dreams.' It was a simple statement but contained a lot of potential.

I made a quick note on my tablet. 'Can you expand please... Sorry, I didn't get your name.'

'Yes, sorry. It's Karen Gilbert.' She paused as I made another note. 'For a month or more now, I have been waking in my bed to the sound of someone singing. There is a man sitting in the chair by my dressing table and he is singing Mr Sandman by the Chordettes. Singing or humming as if he doesn't know all the words. The dream is always the same and I can't move.'

I was typing fast to keep up. 'You cannot move? Are you strapped down or otherwise pinned in place?'

'No,' she shook her head. 'No, I just can't move. It's like I have been drugged or something. I can speak though, just about anyway, but the man never answers.'

'What does the man look like?'

'Old. Like maybe sixty, with grey hair but I can't see all that well because the lights are off and I am lying down meaning I have to squint down my nose to see him. I think he has a phone in his hand because there is a light playing onto his face. Otherwise, I wouldn't be able to see him at all.'

She stopped speaking again so I asked a question, 'How often has this happened? How many times over what period and when did it first happen?' I realized I had just thrown in multiple questions, which I was certain was a poor interview technique, but I stayed quiet to let her answer them all.

She swallowed and glanced at the coffee machine. I followed her eyes, looking at it just as the little green light flicked on to announce its readiness. 'I could do with a coffee,' I said getting up. 'Can I get you one?' The coffee I bought in the coffee shop was still sitting untouched on my desk. I would reheat it later maybe. The Danish pastry was also over there laughing at me while my stomach gurgled its emptiness, but I wasn't going to deal with my needs while I had a client here.

'Um, yes. Thank you,' she replied though I had already picked up a cup for each of us.

'Then, I think we should move to my office,' I stated. It wasn't my office, of course. I was going to use Amanda's, but telling the woman I was just the admin assistant wasn't going to imbue her with a sense of confidence, so I glossed over that detail. 'Just in case someone else comes in.' I added for clarity. PC Van Doorn was going to arrive at some point, but anyone coming in would effectively end our conversation so moving was prudent.

With a coffee in each hand and my tablet tucked under an arm, I ushered her into Amanda's office at the back of the building. Over the next thirty minutes I extracted all the detail she had to give me. The first dream occurred a little more than a month ago and at the time she had awoken the following morning to assume it was nothing but a dream. When it happened a second time a few days later, she dismissed it again though she admitted it felt odd that the dream was exactly the same. A few days later, it happened yet again and that time she woke the next morning in a complete panic and started looking for evidence that someone really had been in her room.

Reporting it to the police had no positive effect as they took a statement but effectively dismissed her. That was two weeks ago, and the *dream* had occurred four times since and then again last night. When she called the police at six o'clock this morning, they sent a squad car to her house. In her words, they were sympathetic but dismissive. 'I get it,' she said. 'I sound like a crazy woman because no matter how I describe it, it sounds like I have had a bad dream. There's no evidence that anyone was there, and I am not reporting an attack. I can't sleep there again though and I didn't know where else to go. My sister lives in Dudley. I can go there but it's a four-hour drive so I can't be there when I have to go to work on Monday.'

Karen stared at me expectantly. While she was speaking, I had listened, asked questions and made notes. That was the easy bit. Now, she expected a response from me, and I had butterflies in my stomach like never before. Did Tempest ever feel like this? I decided the answer was probably not, but whether he did or not, I was here alone and though I felt like a fake, I wasn't going to admit the truth now. I set the tablet down on the table. 'Karen, I believe we can help you,' I said, not really believing a word of it. 'I want you to return to your house. I will visit you after lunch today and will bring some equipment with me.'

'Is that to measure for ghost energy, or something?' she interrupted. I gave her a curious look. 'It's a ghost, isn't it? The old man in the chair by my dressing table. He's the ghost of someone that used to live in the house. I figure he doesn't mean me any harm because he's had plenty of chance to hurt me if he wanted to. Do you have a way to get rid of him?'

I shook my head to clear it. 'The equipment will be to record what is happening in your room. Has the man ever appeared two nights in a row?'

'Um... no,' she answered, confirming what she had already told me.

'Then it seems unlikely he will visit tonight. Do you have any idea how he might be getting into your house? Does anyone have a spare key? Did you change the locks when you moved in?'

Now it was her turn to squint at me. 'He's a ghost, isn't he? Surely he is always there and manifests when he wants to or when triggered by something else.' Her jaw dropped open. 'Oh, my goodness. Have I made this happen?'

How on earth did Tempest deal with the delirium without going nuts. 'Karen...' Just then the door to the main office opened. I hadn't shut Amanda's door, somehow keeping it open made it feel like we were just popping in for a moment; closing the door made it feel like I was invading her space, but when I saw PC Van Doorn closing the main door behind him I got up from behind Amanda's desk. PC Van Doorn threw me a wave and a smile, but I offered him only a curt nod as I closed the inner office door and shut him outside.

'Who was that?' Karen asked.

'A err.... A special consultant from the police. We help them out with their enquiries sometimes,' I lied smoothly. 'Now, Karen. I need to make something clear.'

'Okay,' she said sounding guarded.

'There is no such thing as ghosts.' I let my statement hang in the air for a few seconds to see what her face did. She looked surprised.

'But that means...'

'It means, you are either making the whole thing up. Which I don't believe you are,' I added quickly when she opened her mouth to protest. 'Or, you have a man sneaking into your house at night to sing you a song.'

'Oh, my goodness. That's even worse,' she had a hand to her heart and the other gripped tightly on the arm of her chair as if to anchor herself. 'I can't go back there. I can't.' She looked me in the eye to make sure I knew she meant it.

I nodded my head. I knew what I had to do. 'Karen, do you feel safe there during the day?'

'I guess.'

'Meet me at your house at two o'clock this afternoon. I will set up some recording equipment and dust for prints. I assume the police didn't do that already?'

'No. No, they didn't do anything like that.'

'Then I will. Tonight, I will return to your house and I will lie in wait for your mystery guest. You will have to be there though.' I figured I could stay up a while and sleep in a chair downstairs where I would be disturbed if someone came in. Simon wouldn't like it, but it was what I was going to do. 'First though, I'm afraid I need to go through our fees.' Feeling like I had my feet back on firmer ground, I went through the numbers, something I handled daily for the business. I knew Tempest always did that bit last, making them feel comfortable first and then giving them the confidence that he could solve their problem before telling them what it might cost. It was a tactic that worked as I couldn't remember when a potential client last elected to leave without signing the contract.

Karen was no different but though I was sure Amanda had contract forms in her office, I couldn't find them. I didn't want to rifle through every draw so excused myself to fetch one from my desk.

'Good morning,' I called to PC Van Doorn as I crossed the office. He was sitting with his back to me in the little area by the coffee machine. He swiveled his head to see me. 'Help yourself to coffee. I won't be much longer.' I encouraged him, reaching the desk and vanishing behind it to find the forms I wanted.

'I tried that already,' he laughed. 'I couldn't get it to work. That machine is way too complicated for a cop to figure out.'

I returned his grin. I liked him a lot. 'I'll just wrap up what I am doing and be right with you. It's quite easy once you know how it works.' Then I paused because I was about to say his name and realized I didn't know it. 'I can't keep calling you PC Van Doorn. I need a first name.'

'Jan,' he replied, saying it with a Y so it came out as Yan.

'I won't be long,' I said again as I hurried back to Karen in Amanda's office.

In ten minutes, the forms were signed, and she was getting up to leave. 'So, you are coming at two o'clock?' she asked.

'Yes.'

'I'll meet you there. I'm a little freaked out by it all so I'll be waiting in the car.' I felt a little sorry for her; she was too scared to go into her own house and I wondered how much of that was down to me convincing her that it was a real man and not a ghost. It was an odd case, that was for sure, but she was willing to pay for my investigation and that made her a client.

I let her out of the front door and turned to face Jan. 'Coffee then?'

'Yes, please.' The grin, that seemed a perpetual fixture on his face, stayed in place as I showed him how the machine worked and when I handed over the tiny cup of steaming espresso.

He put his nose over the cup and took a deep sniff. 'Wow! That smells strong.'

I chuckled at his antics. 'You better believe it. I had three one morning and I swear I could smell colours.'

My comment made him laugh, a hearty rumble I found infectious. As he tipped his head back to guffaw, I found myself checking him out; he was tall, with lean limbs that suggested strength but not an abundance of muscle. His arms made me wonder what it might be like to be wrapped up in them and with that I glanced at his groin, the bulge in his jeans keeping my attention for a moment too long because I was still blatantly staring at his package when he brought his head back to level.

I blushed, going deep scarlet beneath my makeup and I looked away, quickly changing the subject to hide my embarrassment. 'Is that the case file?' I asked.

He let me off the hook about his package thankfully, pretending it had never happened as he relaxed back into one of the chairs. He put the coffee down and picked up the folder. It was exactly that in the very sense of the word and for me it was like being transported back to my father's office in the late nineties where they were still using bits of paper and seemed terrified of the computers they had bought.

'Are you expecting any more clients?' he asked as I opened the cardboard outer case and started to inspect the contents.

I replied without looking up, 'I wasn't expecting that one actually. She walked in when I opened up.' The folder contained police reports and photographs, forensic reports and details of interviews. There was a lot to read. 'This is going to take me a while to get through,' I said looking up. 'Are you familiar with the contents?'

'The cases? Yeah, I know all about them. I think that's why Chief Inspector Quinn assigned me to be your liaison. What do you want to know?'

'Let's start with who the two victims were and how they came to be at the lake.'

'Okay, well, the two cops were Martin Gregory and Craig Farnell. Martin was thirty-four years old, divorced and living with his mum. It was his mum that reported his absence when he didn't come home for two days and she couldn't raise him on the phone. She said it wasn't unusual for him to stay out for the night because he would meet girls and she didn't like him bringing them back to the house. Craig was thirty-seven, also divorced, his birthday occurred two days before his body was found and he went missing on the night of his birthday. Martin lived in Ashford; he took a promotion to detective sergeant last year and transferred to an open position. Craig lived in Lenham.'

'Neither one had any good reason to be out near Biddenden Lake then? It's nowhere near their homes.'

'Exactly. Quite what they were doing there or how they got there remains a mystery. Their cars were found at their home addresses.'

Jan and I talked on for an hour as I pieced together a picture of their last movements. Martin was found by a Labrador out with its owner for a long Sunday walk. The owner, Mrs Faversham, called the dog to come away believing he had found some discarded clothing. Only when it refused to obey did she amble over to see what the dog was obsessed by. When Craig went missing a few weeks later, CI Quinn sent a squad car to the lake to have a look just in case.'

I asked, 'Does he think someone is going after police officers? Or is it just coincidence?'

Jan shrugged. 'I doubt we can rule anything out. What I do know is that the chief inspector is under a serious amount of pressure to solve this. While I am here with you, there is a lot of other resource working on this elsewhere.'

I placed the contents of the file back inside the cardboard folder and closed it. I would go through it in more detail later. 'Are you staying with me all day?' I asked the delicious young policeman as I tried hard not to think of him in such terms.

'That's my job,' he replied, once again hitting me with a smile that went straight to my groin. I was going to have to tell him I was a boy at some point soon. The poor guy was flirting with me in a very subtle and flattering way and I didn't want it to stop though I knew no good could come of it.

'I need to visit someone. A business around the corner actually. Then I have to ditch you after lunch to work on another case and I will be working tonight and having a late start tomorrow in all likelihood.'

'Ooh, what's the case?' he asked in an engaging way. We were both on our feet and heading to the door.

'Creepy old man sneaking into a woman's bedroom and singing to her at night. I also think he is drugging her somehow.'

'Wow! What's he singing?'

Surprised by the question, because of all the things I might want to know, the name of the tune wasn't one of them, I told him anyway.

'Never heard of it,' he concluded. 'Where are we going anyway?'

'Here,' I said, pointing up to a sign above our heads. We had walked no more than about sixty yards and turned the corner by the ancient Northgate that was once the entrance to the city.

He followed my finger. 'Mystery Men? It looks like a bookshop.'

The door at the bottom was open as usual, but it led immediately to a set of stairs to take us up to the next floor where the quaint little bookshop sat on the first floor. Framed pictures of aliens, the Loch Ness Monster and other conspiracies adorned the walls on both sides, Jan paused to look at them as we climbed. 'What is this place?' he murmured quietly.

I didn't answer. Instead, I pushed through the door, the little bell above my head jingling excitedly to announce customers to the people within. Not unusually for a Saturday morning, the shop was busy, lots of teenage boys buying comics and three girls with black and blue hair, fishnets tights, lots of leather and too much black makeup were perusing horror movies. I always felt like the shop attracted stereotypes as all I ever saw were geeks and grungy emos. I had to wonder what they made of me in my immaculate office wear.

Poison, the young Chinese shop assistant was serving at the counter. I caught her eye when she looked over. 'Is Frank in?' I asked, raising my voice so I could be heard over the general chatter and the weird-looking science fiction film Frank had playing on a big screen tv.

'He's in the back getting something,' she replied between transactions. I figured she meant for us to wait though it was often hard to tell with Poison. She had an edgy, dangerous kind of character with an attitude to match. It wasn't that she was rude ever, she just didn't seem to want to engage with anyone or be friendly. I knew one thing about her; the boys that came into the shop, came in just to see her half the time. She was nineteen or maybe twenty and had the body of a ballerina mixed with a martial arts master; all lean and hard and capable looking.

I stood to one side with Jan behind me but seconds later I could hear Frank's voice echoing through from behind the counter. What I knew about Frank was that Tempest liked to ask him questions. He was the polar opposite of Tempest though, believing fervently that everything paranormal, supernatural, weird or unexplained was absolutely real and most likely doubted because of a government cover up.

'You got company,' drawled Poison to Frank, flicking her head towards me as she dealt with the next customer.

He turned his head to see who it was, peering over the top of his glasses. 'Won't be a moment,' he offered me a quick grin, then turned back to the person waiting for the large box he held. The two men exchanged some hushed words just off to one side of the counter and away from everyone else. Then they shook hands, but not in the normal grip and shake once way that people do. They clasped hands then rotated their elbows and both looked to the sky and crossed themselves with their free hand. The man had the box tucked under one arm but still managed to perform the maneuver. Like I said before: In a world of weird in which I operate, Frank sat near the top of the scale.

With a final nod at Frank, the man left via the stairs, the treads creaking under his weight as he descended.

'Now, what can I do for you today, Miss Jane? No Tempest?'

'Hello, Frank. Tempest is in France tackling a Yeti.'

'A Yeti?' Frank interrupted. 'Ursus Petram, the Himilayan rock bear? Odd for it to have travelled as far as France but it's not the first time.'

From behind me, Jan said, 'Um?'

'Frank this is PC Jan Van Doorn. He is a special police liaison for a case the agency is working on. I am getting started in Tempest's absence.'

Frank extended his hand which Jan took with only a quick glance to make sure it was human and not webbed or reptilian or something. 'Please to meet you, Jan. Now how can I help you pair? It's what I do, after all. Honestly, I'm sure it wouldn't kill Tempest to buy something once in a while. I recognise my place though and I am always ready to assist where I can, fighting the forces of evil that threaten to invade our plane of existence.'

Before Frank could get into full rant mode, I said, 'What do you know about a swamp monster at Biddenden Lake?'

He stopped speaking and blinked at me behind his glasses; once, twice. 'You are referring to the recent *drownings* there?' he asked making the quotation sign in the air with both hands when he said drownings.

Jan was startled by his response. 'How can you possibly know anything about that? The whole case has been kept completely under wraps.'

Frank whipped out a Dictaphone from a pocket just as I spun around to clamp a hand over Jan's mouth. 'Can you say that again, please?' asked Frank. 'Specifically, the bit about the cover up where uniformed agents of the government try to block the truth from reaching the public.'

I looked over my shoulder at him. 'Put it away, please, Frank,' To stop Jan from speaking, I had to get right inside his personal space and now there was a lot of me touching a lot of him and I was reluctant to step back. I wanted to lay my head on his chest and breath in his cologne.

Reluctantly, and with some grumpy noises, Frank put the recording device back into a pocket. 'You cannot deny that I just heard him claim a cover up, Jane. You know as well as I that these creatures are out there, and the public are unable to properly defend themselves because they are misled. You used to be a vampire, for goodness sake.'

Jan prised my hand away from his mouth. 'You used to be a vampire. What on earth is going on here?'

Blushing beneath my makeup, I turned back to face Frank, letting Jan go in the process. 'I'll tell you about it later,' I said over my shoulder. 'Frank, the swamp monster?'

'Oh, yes. Well, there was a lot of discussion when this first occurred because someone in my community suggested it could be mermaids. The bite marks are close in radius and teeth pattern to those a mermaid inflicts. The similarities end there though.'

'Mermaids?' said Jan.

Frank spared him a very quick glance but didn't stop talking. 'Mermaids are strictly saltwater inhabitants. First reported by Captain Otto Schneider in 1746, whose whaling ship, the Dominico, was stranded at sea in four days of doldrums. Running out of fresh water, his crew began to report strange voices singing to them from the still waters. The siren song, a term which wasn't coined for another fifty years, lured almost half his ship's company to their graves though they managed to capture one in a net as the remaining crew fought for their lives. The mermaid cut itself free using a crude knife made of seashell, but the legend was born.' Frank had a faraway look in his eyes as if pondering the majesty of seeing these mythical creatures for himself.

I thought I would need to prompt him for more but the bell above the door tinkled again and the noise brought him back to reality. The person coming in didn't pass in front of me so must have turned left to look at the books at the back of the shop. Frank spared the person a glance, blinked his glazed eyes and started talking again. 'Anyway, what you have in Biddenden Lake is a nasty case of water sprites, otherwise known as category three water demons. They can be nasty little horrors and they revel in causing harm.'

'That sounds like a load of old tosh,' said a worryingly familiar voice from right by the door. I turned my head to discover that the person who had just entered hadn't turned left at all, she had merely stopped moving so she could listen to our conversation. She saw my opened-mouthed stare and shot me a grin that was full of false teeth.

When I found my voice, I asked, 'Gran? What are you doing here?'

'Well, I phoned your house to see if you would like to meet for lunch today, but your boyfriend; oh, he's ever such a nice chap, well, he said you were working today. So, I got on the bus, well, you know it stops right outside my house and I get a free bus pass on account of my age. Anyway, it comes direct to Rochester High Street, it's only seven stops and takes less than twenty minutes, you know. So, I found your office, ooh, it's ever so fancy. I couldn't see it properly because it was locked but I had a peer through the windows: very nice.'

My grandmother was in full on old-lady-description and anecdote mode. If I didn't stop her, we would get a full run down of what the bus driver looked like and how she thought he needed a haircut. 'Gran,' I tried fruitlessly. 'Gran,' I interrupted again but it was like throwing acorns in front of a road roller. 'GRANDMOTHER.' This time, my raised voice broke through the sound of her own voice to penetrate her chain of thought.

'What is it, dear? I was just going to tell you about the lady in the coffee shop. She told me where to look for you.' Gran looked grumpy now, but she had been talking for two minutes straight while the rest of us stood silent.

'I'm working, gran. I don't have time for lunch.'

Jan nudged my arm. 'We will have to eat at some point. I'm sure we can accommodate stopping for a bite to eat with this lovely lady,' he said while giving my gran a hearty grin.

Gran gave him an appreciative once over. 'Ooh, you're nice. I'm a bit old for you though love. You should stick to ladies your own age.'

'No, I, ah, I meant,' Jan tried, but gran had already stopped listening.

She was staring at Frank instead. 'So, what were you saying about water demons, young man. If my Jane is going to solve another crime, I want to know all about it.'

Frank, wondering if he might be allowed to speak, didn't say anything for a few seconds. Then, with all three of us looking at him, he started talking again. 'Right. Well, yes, you are dealing with water demons at Biddenden Lake. It's not the first time either. Not that we get many cases, but you needn't worry, the Kent League of Demonologists will take care of them.'

'What?' said Jan, screwing his face up as he tried to get his head around Frank's last statement. 'I got lost there somewhere. I don't understand anything about what is going on. Jane used to be a vampire, this shop seems to operate in an entirely different reality to the rest of the planet and now you have a Kent charter of demon hunters.'

'Kent League of Demonologists,' Frank corrected him.

'Codswollop,' commented gran.

'Can you back up a bit and start again?' Jan asked.

Frank pursed his lips. 'How far back do you want me to go?'

Jan rubbed his forehead. 'From hello, I think. After that it all seems fuzzy.'

Frank didn't start again though. Instead, he turned around to speak with Poison. 'Poison, dear, can you get the reality-shaken juice, please?' when he turned back to me, he saw the curious look on my face. 'We get this sometimes. People believe they have a firm grip on reality and then discover that most of what they believe isn't real. It shakes them to their core and can make them spiral if not treated quickly enough.'

Poison came from behind the counter with an ancient-looking hip flask. It looked to be made from pewter, but it had a leather binding around it that looked more like alligator skin. She was wearing a glove to hold it and had another glove for Frank to put on before she passed it to him.

Then she took off her glove and passed it to Frank, who in turn offered it to Jan.

'What's this?' he asked staring at the glove he now held.

Frank paused with the glove in one hand and the flask in the other. 'The flask is coated in dragon hide. It's perfectly safe to work and touch right after the dragon has been slain, but a few years later it begins to take on magical properties and can burn your skin on contact. A quick swig of this will see you right though.'

'I don't think so. What the heck is it anyway? Vampire's blood? Juice fermented from the brain of a werewolf? Zombie spit?'

Jan was being flippant, but Frank said, 'How can it be vampire blood? They don't have any. It's the accelerant found in a dragon's firesac. It's what ignites when it breathes fire.'

Jan fixed him with a disbelieving look. 'Really?'

Frank flipped his eyebrows. 'No, not really. It's whiskey. Good stuff too. So have a drop and shut up before I change my mind.'

When Jan hesitated, gran made a grab for the flask. 'I'll have some, thank you.' The dragon skin on the flask didn't hiss and scald her hand when she touched it, but Frank made a dive for it anyway as she put up a hand to ward him off and took a healthy belt of scotch. 'Cor, that's better,' she announced as she handed it back. 'I can feel that warming my toes.'

'Crikey,' said Frank as he held up the flask once more. 'It's half empty. Is she going to be alright?'

'Compared to what?' I shrugged despairingly.

This was becoming quite the pantomime. I checked my watch to find it was approaching noon. I needed to get on with things so I could keep my two o'clock appointment with Karen Gilbert.

'Thank you, Frank,' I offered my hand to shake as I moved toward the door. 'I think we have taken up enough of your time.' Jan was following but I had to give gran a bit of a shove to get her moving and grab her shoulders to turn her around.

She was too busy looking about, trying to see all there was to see in the bookshop. 'This is a very odd place, you know,' she commented as I managed to get her through the door. 'It reminds me of the first time I went into one of those sex shops back in the seventies. Mavis Gowling dared me to go in and buy something. Well, I was shocked by what I found in there, but I bought myself an enormous...'

Mercifully, Frank called out a final piece of advice to drown out what she said next. 'Remember to use salt. Water sprites hate salt,' he said in a loud voice so we would hear him over the noise of the traffic outside.

I raised a thumbs up above my head as I swung out of the bottom door.

Lunch. Saturday, December 3rd 1227hrs

SATURDAY IN ROCHESTER IS not the time to look for somewhere to eat lunch if you haven't reserved a table. Yes, there are lots of places to eat, but there are also lots of tourists flocking in from Europe on the nearby high-speed train line, plus citizens from the local towns descend upon the picturesque High Street every weekend. Had it been one of the many festival weekends, we would not have stood a chance, but we lucked out on the fourth attempt with an Italian place.

My attempts to discourage Jan from staying with me for the cringe-worthy event with my gran were to no avail. He claimed he was hungry and said my gran was funny. She could be funny, but I wasn't sure that this was going to be one of those times. The whisky had indeed warmed her toes, but on the way down it made her legs drunk and she was swaying from side to side as she followed the waiter through the tables.

'Sorry,' she said as she bumped a table with a hip. 'Sorry,' again as she bumped the next one. 'The floor in here could be a bit more even, you know,' she complained to the waiter as we reached our table.

'I'm sorry?' he said, confused by her comment.

'I should think so, young man. Tell the owner to get a builder in to look at it.' The poor man shot me a questioning look to which I just shook my head and gave him a grimace that suggested she was a getting a little senile.

40

Settled in our chairs, he handed out menus and left us with the advice that Sarah would be our server. Jan excused himself to head to the gents and I took the opportunity to ask gran why she had decided to find me today.

'Well, dear,' she started. 'I decided that I miss having you around. After all the nonsense with the vampires I was glad to see the back of you; it'll be years before my geraniums grow back properly. I could do with a hand around the house though. I'm eighty-four after all. So, I just wanted to say that if you were to need somewhere to stay, you can have your old room back. Or the basement if that is what you prefer.'

This was a surprise. I didn't need a place to stay but had lived with my gran since I was thirteen and her place felt like home. My parents weren't dead, they weren't even divorced. They just weren't very good parents, so I had been lucky to have a grandmother who was prepared to take me in. I had to acknowledge though that I deserved to be kicked out when it happened. At the time, I was deep into the pretend vampire lifestyle and had begun to treat her place like it was my own and could be taken for granted.

I placed my hand on top of hers. 'Thank you, gran. That's very kind of you. I don't need a place right now, but it would be nice to come and visit you again.'

'I thought so,' she replied kindly. Then the serious look left her face as she glanced around the restaurant. 'Where's that lazy waitress? I need a drink.'

'Shouldn't we wait for Jan?'

'Nah, stuff him. I'm an old lady. He will be just fine.' As if forgetting her quest for more alcohol, she looked back at me and gave me an appraising once over. 'I have to say that you are much prettier as a girl than you ever were as a boy.'

'Um, thank you. I think.'

'It's so nice that you are one of those homosexuals now.'

Startled by her statement, I glanced about to see who was looking. 'Is it?'

'Oh, yes. All the other ladies at bingo have a grandson or a granddaughter who is gay or lesbian or something different. I have been the odd one out for too long. I used to boast that you were a vampire, but they just laughed at that. Since you came out, I have been able to join in the conversations properly. And then, well, when you started dressing as a girl, I became the queen bee. No one else has a transgender homosexual in their family. Hah! Top that Doris Halfpenny.'

'What are you ladies talking about?' asked Jan as he retook his seat. The waitress arrived to take our order though, so the question never got answered and our conversation turned to what case I was working on right now. I told gran about Arthur the ogre and then about the swamp monster making sure I kept away from any details because of the non-disclosure agreement.

The drinks arrived first; diet coke for me, water for Jan and a double gin and tonic for gran. I was going to have to drop her home. There was no way I could put her on a bus; she might end up anywhere.

'You keep checking the time, dear,' observed gran halfway through her meal. It is a point worth noting that it was halfway through her meal but not halfway through mine or Jan's. Gran ate slow.

'I have an appointment at two o'clock, gran. I don't want to be late.'

'Well, don't let me keep you, dear,' she replied around another mouthful of pasta. Looking across at my plate and then Jan's she realized we were finished and waiting for her. Sighing she put her knife and fork down. 'It's these infernal teeth,' she said. 'They won't stay still so chewing takes ages. I don't bother with them at home half the time.' Then, just like that, she reached into her mouth and popped out both sets of dentures. 'Parsh me that glarsh, love,' she pointed across the table.

Jan's eyes were widened in mute horror as he watched the teeth plop into the glass of water. Then, scooping up her cutlery once more, a fresh mouthful of pasta went in.

'Thatsss, mush better,' she announced as she chewed with renewed vigour while Jan and I tried to ignore the bits of half-chewed pasta falling from her dentures to the bottom of the glass.

Gran didn't bother to look up when she said, 'It'll happen to you as well, deary. Everyone getsh old.' Sage advice indeed, but I checked my watch again and raised an arm to signal the waitress.

'I'll get this,' volunteered Jan.

'Nonsense,' I replied and the inevitable tussle over who would pay for what raged for a few seconds until gran reached into her purse to produce a wad of fifty-pound notes.

'I'll get lunch. That's the other thing about getting old, dear: you haven't got much to spend your money on anymore. It's not like I get to go clubbing and need to buy new shoes every week.'

The waitress took the cash away and returned with gran's change, however, my hope that I might now get her moving and be able to get to Karen's house were dashed when she announced a need to use the ladies and requested my help.

As I helped gran from her chair, I turned to Jan. 'You should go. I have tasks to perform this afternoon and probably tonight, but I will be doing research into your case in between them. I'll call tomorrow if I have any questions or need your help with anything, okay?'

'Yeah, sure,' Jan replied with his usual wide smile. 'This was a fun lunch, but you're going to have to explain about how you used to be vampire at some point.' He said it with a smile, curious about me but not sure what to make of all the weird that revolved around my life. He hesitated for a moment, looking at my face as if trying to work out whether to shake my hand or something. The voice in my head told me he wanted to ask me out but hadn't plucked up the courage for that yet. I was going to have to tell him I wasn't a girl before he did. Now wasn't the time though.

He settled on giving me a quick wave, said, 'See you later, Jane Butterworth,' and was gone, leaving me to deal with gran. Fortunately, the only help she wanted with her trip to the ladies was finding it. Waiting for her to come back out ticked away too much of my remaining time though, so when she was ready, I unhappily accepted that in order to keep my appointment with Karen Gilbert, I would have to take Gran with me.

This was going to be embarrassing.

Karen Gilbert's House. Saturday, December 3rd 1400hrs

'Where is it we are going again?' gran asked for the third or fourth time.

'To a client's house. She has a man disturbing her sleep.'

'Hah! Does she really?' cackled my grandmother from the passenger's seat. 'There a word for girls like that.'

I sighed, worrying that this afternoon might be more painful than it needed to be. 'No, gran. The man is getting into her house uninvited. She hired me to find out how he is doing it and why, and then to find a way to stop him.'

'Stop him?'

'Yes, gran. That part will probably involve the police, but I need to identify the person and gather sufficient evidence for the police to respond first.'

Gran turned in her seat to look at me, paying attention for once. 'Why don't they investigate?'

It was a valid question. 'Because at this point, there is no perceivable crime. The police have no evidence that anything has happened. The man hasn't harmed her, but he is freaking her out.'

'What's he doing?'

'He sings to her.'

'That sounds nice,' gran said with a smile.

I rolled my eyes. 'The poor woman wakes up in the night to find a strange man sitting in her bedroom singing her Mr Sandman. I wouldn't find it nice. It would scare the crap out of me.'

'Yes, well, it's been a while since I had a man in my room. Strange or not,' gran said with a wistful look in her eyes. 'The Sandman. That's what you should call him.' It was as good a name as any and I doubted I would now be able to think of him by any other.

Moments later I stopped my car outside the address Karen gave me. It was a pretty cottage in rural Kent and had a real fire inside unless the smoke rising from the chimney was a clever bluff. Red London brick surrounded small windows set equidistance either side of the centrally-set front door, and rose bushes, clipped for the winter, grew on wood trellis right up to the upper story windows. It looked delightful, almost like something from a story, though for the occupant, right now the story was one from a horror book.

I hoped I could help her with that.

With the engine off, I went around to gran's side and helped her out, then, walking slowly as gran hobbled along with her walking stick, we set off down the garden path.

'This is nice,' said gran.

'It looks a lot like your cottage, gran.'

'No, I mean getting out. I don't get out much. Bingo twice a week, of course, and I have afternoon tea with the ladies from the women's institute every Thursday. But I don't get out in the country like this anymore. Thank you for bringing me.'

It was nice of gran to thank me. Okay, I didn't have much option and she was sharp as a tack so had probably engineered things at the restaurant so I had to bring her with me, but she was my gran and far more maternal than my mother had ever been.

I was smiling to myself about her as we neared the house, but the door opened before we got to it. Karen appeared, an anxious look dominating her face. 'I was worried you weren't coming.'

'I'm right on time, am I not?' I knew I was because I checked the clock a dozen times on the way over.

'Yes, yes. Sorry. I'm just nervous about being back in the house. I know it's irrational; it's daylight after all. But, well...'

I raised a hand to stop her. 'It's perfectly alright. I'm sure I would be feeling unsettled if this were happening to me. I brought equipment with me,' I said, holding up a backpack. Tempest kept gear in lockers in the storage area of the office building and a couple of backpacks so he and Amanda could easily stuff things in and go when they needed to. Some of the items I wanted had gone with him to France but there was enough left for this case.

'This is my gran, by the way,' I said aloud, then dropped my voice to a soft whisper. 'I don't usually have her with me. She came by the office and I didn't have time to drop her off and still get there on time. I hope you don't mind.'

Karen gave me an awkward smile which I took to mean she has a gran too. 'Shall I make tea?' she asked, looking at my gran rather than me.

'That would be nice, dear. I'm Vera. Vera Cambridge. Is there somewhere I can sit while James gets on with his business?' I froze, wondering if this was going to lead to an awkward conversation.

'James?' asked Karen, her brow wrinkling in confusion.

'Sorry. Sorry, I meant Jane. I do get myself confused.' Karen politely assumed that my grandmother was just getting a bit iffy in the mental arena and led her through to her tiny cottage lounge where an armchair and a large ginger cat awaited.

Remaining in the hallway, I started talking as Karen came back out, 'I have some questions, Karen, if you are ready?'

'Of course. I'll just put the kettle on.' Karen went around me and through a door on the other side of the hall. I followed her into what turned out to be a small galley kitchen. A window provided a view over a lovely garden. A feeder full of seed hung in front of the window with birds pecking hungrily at it. They burst into the air as one when I looked at them. 'What it is you would like to know?' Karen asked as she took the kettle to the sink.

'I need you to show me your bedroom so I can set up a pair of cameras and the seat he was sitting in so I can dust for prints. I doubt he will have left prints on the door handles, but I will check. What I want to ask you about is your neighbours, work colleagues etcetera. If this man has targeted you specifically, my assumption is that he knows you from somewhere. He might live down the street or be a man that sees you each week at the supermarket.'

'You really think this is a person and not some disquiet spirit. Mr Bagatus gets antsy sometimes and I always thought it was because he could detect an evil presence.'

For clarity I needed to ask a question, 'Mr Bagatus is the cat?'

'Yes. Yes, sorry, I should have introduced him, shouldn't I?'

While the kettle boiled on her gas stove, I took out the finger-printing kit and asked her for a full set of prints; I needed to be sure I was looking at ones that were not hers. Then, I set about dusting the frame and handle around the back door. 'Does anyone else have a key?'

'No. Well, my mum does.'

'I want you to check she still has it please. Do that now, if you will.' I waited while she used her phone to send a quick text message. 'How long ago did you move in please? And who was the previous tenant?'

'I...' her phone beeped to interrupt what she planned to say. 'Mum says the key is hanging where it always hangs: in her utility room. I moved in six years ago, but the previous occupants were a couple that lived here for sixty-three years

48

and died of old age. They were known to the family, so I got the house cheap before it even went on the market.'

'I need to see your bedroom,' I said, slipping items back into the pack that came with the fingerprint kit.

Just then there was a crashing noise from elsewhere in the house. Karen and I glanced at each other, then we both moved at once, Karen pausing only to put down the cup of tea she had for my grandmother.

Dashing into the lounge, I feared I might find that gran had fallen over. It was just her walking stick though, which had fallen from her hands to knock into the small rack of brass tools set by the fireplace. The sound we heard was several of them falling off.

Gran was asleep.

Or possibly dead. Honestly, it was hard to tell.

Coming into the room behind me, Karen said, 'Is she okay?'

I opened my mouth to give a flippant reply, but gran chose that moment to snort out a loud snore. Well, she wasn't dead at least, that would have made the afternoon less productive. Karen put the walking stick against a nearby sideboard before following me back out of the room.

Upstairs, I dusted for more prints, particularly underneath her dressing table stool and on the edge of the dressing table where I hoped he might have placed a hand. There was nothing though. He either wore gloves or he was very careful. Climbing off my knees where I had been crouched beneath her dressing table, I crossed the room to pull her curtains together.

'What are you doing?' Karen asked.

Grimacing because I didn't want to explain it, I said, 'I need to perform one final check.' Then I took out a blacklight and a pair of goggles.

When I switched it on, she gasped, 'Oh, my goodness. You're checking for... for...'

'Yes, I'm checking to make sure he wasn't leaving little knuckle children on your carpet,' I helpfully filled in her blanks.

Karen said, 'Ewwww,' and did a little unhappy dance as if she felt covered in lice or something. Thankfully, we both got to see that there were no telltale signs of liquid on her bedroom floor. I think we were both relieved, her more than me obviously, but when the light flooded back in through the curtains, she asked, 'What next?'

I had to think about that for a while. 'I am going to set up a pair of cameras, if you will give me permission. It will mean I have recorded material of you in your bedroom. You can have it all back or watch me destroy it, or you can just say no, but I want to see if I can catch him with an infrared camera. I also want to stay here overnight.' It was something I knew Tempest had done in the past. If he thought a criminal might strike, it could often be the fastest way to bring a case to its conclusion.

Karen Gilbert looked at the floor as she thought about what I had asked her to agree to, mulling things over probably. When she looked back up though, she didn't agree to my request. Instead, she had a question of her own. 'How will you stop him?' she looked at me for second before adding. 'I mean, I don't know how big he is, but he's not a small man. I wouldn't want to tackle him. If you stay here at night, what will you do if he turns up? Call the police? The nearest station is Maidstone. It will take them half an hour to get this far out into the countryside.'

I got what she was saying: I presented her with the image of a reasonably tall, but nevertheless petite woman. I weigh just a little more than one hundred pounds so I can't use my weight against anyone either. I wasn't going to tell her I was a man because it really wouldn't make any difference to my ability to overpower the Sandman. However, it might very well completely change her thinking on whether I was allowed to film her in bed at night though.

I decided to lie. 'I'm trained in martial arts. If he turns up, he'll soon find he has a mouthful of carpet and a small blonde woman making one of his elbows touch his ear.'

With a perplexed frown, Karen lifted an arm, twisting it around in a bid to work out how I could get an elbow anywhere near his head. She gave up. 'Okay, well, that answered my question. I don't want to put any pressure on you, but I'm not staying here tonight unless you are here too.'

'Oh.' Simon wasn't going to like this. 'I thought he had never come two nights in a row?'

'He hasn't so far. I'm not going to risk it though. I want you to catch him and prove I'm not going nuts. You can put the cameras up, as many of them as you like, in fact. But I'm not going to be here at night without you here as well. Can you do that?'

I didn't feel like I had much choice. I wanted to see what it was like to be an investigator and this was it. This was my chance to give it a go. If I could solve this case, then maybe I could solve other cases. Karen was right to ask the question about how I would subdue the man, actual fight training something I had already considered because I recognized it was a weak area for me.

Slowly, I nodded. 'I need to take gran home and I need to attend to some other tasks, but I can be back here later this evening.'

Karen bit her lip. 'I, ah, I don't have guests very often. Shall I get a bottle of wine?'

I knew the answer to this just from listening to Amanda and Tempest talk about their work and from typing up reports for them. 'No. I'll need to stay sober and alert. I'm afraid this isn't a social visit. I'll enter from the rear of the house under cover of darkness. If the Sandman is watching, I don't want him to see me and change his mind about visiting.'

'Gosh. Yes, good point. I hadn't thought of that. It's clear you've been doing this for years.' I smirked to myself at her comment, feeling it tweak the corners of my mouth. She was looking right at me but didn't react to it. 'So, you'll let me know when you are coming? I'm not staying here by myself, but I will be brave and come back when you say you are on your way.'

'I will do that.' While I spoke, I mentally totted up all the things on my to do list. My diary was getting busy and suddenly top of the list was finding a self-defense class I could attend. You know, just in case the lies I told about being a ninja came back to bite my backside.

Jennifer Lasseter. Saturday, December 3rd 1537hrs

'WHAT DO YOU MEAN you don't know what time you will be home tonight? Are you kidding me right now?' Simon's voice was filled with venom.

'I already told you, Simon: I have a terrified client and I need to see if I can catch her tormentor. It might be late when I get back.'

'It's Saturday night, James,' he snapped back at me, using my real name to inflict injury because he knew I was dressed as Jane. 'What exactly constitutes late on a Saturday night? We often don't get in until two or three in the morning. Sometimes later than that.'

'Well, it might be around that time.' Or even later, I didn't add. I wasn't expecting the Sandman to turn up, but would it be fair on Karen for me to decide at three that he wasn't coming and leave. What if he turned up ten minutes after I drove away?

Simon wasn't done asking questions though. 'What is with you, babe?' At least his voice had softened. 'You've always been such a party girl. Now you want to pretend you are a detective. I get it; you've got a crush on your boss. I'm not jealous. I just think this is a silly waste of time. You are the admin assistant. When did you suddenly learn to be an investigator? Have you been watching late night episodes of Mike Hammer?'

He knew I was a fan of that show, but he wasn't being fair. I had sprung this on him and ruined his plan for the weekend, but so what? It wasn't like we were doing anything special. Drinks in town, something to eat and then off to a club until the small hours. What Simon failed to grasp was that where he had found his career and was succeeding, I was still searching for definition.

I didn't know how to say all that, so I said, 'I'm sorry,' for the umpteenth time.

'You're sorry,' Simon echoed. 'So, you won't change your mind. You're going to let me and all our friends down for some silly mission.'

'I'll be home as early as I can.'

I got a final, 'Don't rush,' and he put the phone down on me. He actually hung up. I couldn't believe it. I needed to go by the house later to change clothes and pick up a toothbrush, but his mood was going to make it awkward. I just hoped he wouldn't want to get into another fight.

Huffing to myself, I started toward the address I had for Jennifer Lasseter. I thought about phoning ahead, which was more to ensure she was in and my journey not wasted but dismissed the idea. She would either agree to speak with me, or she wouldn't, but over the phone I had no ability to see how her face reacted to the past being dredged up or what her body language might tell me.

With that in mind, once gran was settled safely back in her house in Aylesford, I set off to visit Jennifer. Like Karen, in fact like lots of people in this part of the county, Jennifer lived in a small village. Not far from Biddenden Lake in nearby village Smarden, Jennifer's address turned out to be a semi-detached house in a winding row of new builds. Houses were still being built in these quiet rural settings, generally against the wishes of the residents in the original village.

Her house was in one such development on the edge of Smarden, but the area had been tastefully built and landscaped so I found it hard to see what everyone complained so bitterly about. People had to live somewhere, surely we couldn't shove all of them into the cities to preserve the rural areas.

I parked in front of her drive, relieved to see there was a car on it. That had to mean there was someone in, right. I knocked on the door, then stood back to wait.

Jennifer's picture was in the case file Jan gave me this morning but lying in bed next to Simon's cold shoulder last night, I had looked at her social media profile and found lots of pictures, so it was easy to recognize her when the door opened.

'Can I help you?' she asked, sounding quietly curious as I was not someone she recognised and not what she expected if I was about to sell her something.

'I'm sorry,' I started, then corrected myself; I wasn't supposed to be apologizing. It felt like a very weak way to lead off. 'Jennifer Lasseter, my name is Jane Butterworth, I have been hired by Kent Police to look into recent deaths at Biddenden Lake. Can I have a few moments of your time?'

The woman looked me up and down, quickly as if assessing me, then stared directly at me. 'Kent Police, huh? You know they made my life hell for months. Now they think I have something to do with the recent deaths, I suppose?'

I shook my head. 'No, nothing like that. I am not here on their behalf. I am just looking to better understand what happened... for perspective in my own investigation.'

She wriggled her mouth around as she considered my request, arriving at a decision a few seconds later. 'You had better come in.'

I squeezed around her as she took a step back to let me in then paused while she closed the door because I didn't know where she would want me to go. She led me through to her living room where she invited me to sit. 'I assume you have a list of questions you'd like to ask?' she said once I was settled and had my tablet poised for taking notes.

It was at this point that I realised I didn't have a question for her. Why was I here? Too late now, I was going to have to bluff my way through it. 'Is that him?' I asked, pointing to a picture on a side table. I already knew that it was because, like everything else, his photograph was in the casefile.

'Yes, that's him,' she said sadly. 'You're going to ask me why I still have a picture of him on display in my house.' She didn't wait for me to answer. 'He was taken from me in the most terrible way. I haven't been able to move on. I haven't had another boyfriend since. So, Ian stays with me. In some small way, we will never be apart.'

I wasn't sure how to respond to that. I was surprised by it, but maybe it was normal for trauma to manifest like this. I didn't know any different. Scrambling for another question, one popped into my head. 'On the morning of his death, you were camping, yes?'

'That's correct.' Her reply added no additional information.

'He had to have left the tent at some point. Did you not notice him leave?'

Jennifer stared at her fingers and then back up at me. 'I woke up when he got out of the sleeping bag, but only briefly. He didn't speak and I assumed he had a call of nature. He left the tent but it was dark and I fell back to sleep without really noticing him go.'

'What time was that?'

'I don't know.' Her answer was laced with impatience. 'It was dark, I barely remember him leaving the tent and I certainly didn't check my watch. When I finally woke up to discover he hadn't returned I went looking for him. That's when I saw the creature and spotted his body in the water.'

'Can you describe the creature for me, please?' I had no particular purpose for my questions, I didn't think she was guilty, but now that I was here, I felt like I had to ask something.

With a quiet tut, Jennifer began to describe the swamp monster. It was standing in the water with everything above its waist showing. It was dark green or possibly grey and had a head a bit like a crocodile. The eyes sat at the front of the face like a human but were large and buggish. She had only seen it for a second in the early morning half-light, but it was long enough for her to memorise what she saw.

56

I pushed forward with another question, one I was sure must have surfaced at the time but the answer to which was not in the information I found so far. 'Prior to his death, you were hospitalized several times. I flicked to the page of notes from last night. 'You broke your right forearm twice, you needed stitches to your lips, your nose was broken, your left cheekbone was broken; all of these were separate incidents. Since his death you haven't suffered a single injury. These look like domestic injuries, Jennifer. Did he beat you?'

Jennifer sighed an exaggerated sigh of boredom. 'The police kept asking the same question three years ago. I got mugged twice, that's what happened to my face. I broke my arm once when I slipped on the decking and Ian broke it once when we got a little bit vigorous in the bedroom. He was mortified that he had managed to hurt me, but it was entirely consensual. I have answered all these questions before, Miss Butterworth. I don't see why I should be subjected to answering them again if I am not a suspect in the latest deaths.'

I couldn't find an argument and had exhausted my hastily thought up list of questions. I shut down my tablet. 'Thank you for your time, Miss Lasseter.'

'You're very welcome,' she replied though she did not sound like she meant it.

With us both standing once more, she escorted me to the door where I collected my coat and slipped it on. It was cold out, but I took my time and made her wait because I came up with another question and wanted to frame it right.

Just as her hand touched the lock to open the door, I asked, 'The creature you saw, the so-called swamp monster, why do you think no one was able to find it?'

A wave of irritation shot across her face, gone as soon as it appeared. 'I couldn't possibly say,' she replied. I saw something and clearly it was there because it came back and has killed again. The papers believed me, why can't the police?'

I extended my hand for her to shake. I had been poking at her to see if there was anything shaky or dubious about her story. There wasn't though. Chief Inspector Quinn still suspected her but his evidence against her seemed circumstantial and superficial.

'Thank you for your time,' I said again and this time I let her open the door for me to leave.

Back outside her house and heading to my car, I considered whether I had learned anything. Jennifer was never brought to trial the first time, which, in my opinion, was most likely because she wasn't guilty. She was a small woman; smaller than me both in height and weight and her boyfriend was a big man. The file Jan gave me contained details about the first victim, Ian Dexter. Photographs from when he was alive and several from his autopsy showed how big he was; a bodybuilder, but one who was also tall and broad naturally. Not that his size was ambiguous because it was listed in the file. He had been six feet three inches tall and weighed two-hundred and thirty-five pounds when he died. Jennifer's lawyer picked the right argument: she couldn't have drowned him.

I checked the time on my phone, but I knew from the darkness now descending that it was getting close to four o'clock. I had a beginners' self-defense class booked at six o'clock, one which offered taster sessions for free and a great picture on their website of old ladies beating up young men.

I would need to go home to grab some clothes for that, but I really didn't feel like dealing with Simon yet. To put off that particular drama, I went to the office instead. Jan's file was there too, and I wanted some peaceful time to go over it carefully.

My hope for a quiet hour or so at the office wasn't to be though.

Frank's Theories. Saturday, December 3rd 1624hrs

FRANK HAMMERED ON THE glass of the office door, peering through it to where I sat at my desk. I had barely made contact with the chair and the coffee machine was still coming up to full working speed, but there he was, his odd little face visible above the frosted portion of the glass.

'Everything okay?' I asked as I unlocked the door.

Frank came in though I hadn't invited him. 'Poison said the light was on. I expected to find Tempest had returned, but it was you I really needed to speak with.'

Curious, I asked, 'Why's that?'

'Witches,' Frank replied while hunching over to look like a withered crone and making his voice sound mysterious. When I didn't react, he waggled his eyebrows mysteriously and when I still didn't react, he gave up and straightened himself to his unimpressive five-foot four-inch height. 'I knew there was something I was forgetting about Biddenden Lake. It came to me this afternoon, but I don't have your number.'

'What about the lake?' I asked, walking over to the coffee machine as the green light flicked on.

'Ooh, is that fresh coffee on offer?' Frank asked, peering around me to see the machine. 'We have terrible coffee at the bookshop.'

I turned to face him. 'Isn't it your shop? Couldn't you just get better coffee?'

Frank pursed his lips. 'Yeah, well, overheads, you know.' I didn't know actually. I got the impression Frank made good money but had no idea what he spent it on. He walked to work even when it was raining so if he owned a car, I had never seen it and he certainly didn't spend the money on clothes because he was scruffier than your average student. I made him a cup anyway, then reloaded the machine for myself.

Sniffing the dark liquid with his nose over the cup and his eyes closed, Frank started telling me why he was excited about Biddenden Lake. 'This area of Kent has been inhabited for many millennia and most of the villages are a thousand years old. Most were named in the Magna Carta, but it's a superstitious area, rightly so, of course, as it is also one of the most haunted places on the planet.'

'Why is that?' I asked.

Frank rolled his eyes. 'Because the villages have been here for so long. So many dead bodies in such close proximity with the living; they were always going to revolt. Witchcraft has been a particular problem. Three hundred years ago, witches in the area were becoming a nuisance. The sensible precaution of keeping to themselves and practicing their magic where others couldn't see had been discarded with more and more of them making themselves public and daring villagers to challenge them. Growing more powerful, they were perceived as dangerous even if avoided and became targets for the terrified townsfolk. Banded together by their leaders in 1690, two years before the Salem Witch Trials, a purge began. Any woman suspected of witchcraft was brought to a place of justice and drowned, the accused forced into a sack weighted down with rocks before being tossed into a lake. One such location these executions took place was...'

'Biddenden Lake,' I finished.

'Yes. The practice stopped though when several of the executed witches reappeared and set fire to all the houses in Biddenden. The legend has it that they returned to the lake after they set the fires, their wet footprints followed by plucky villagers determined to put an end to the terror. Then all the fish in the lake died and anyone that went near the lake was drawn into it and drowned.' Frank's voice had taken on a storyteller's edge. When he finished speaking, I expected a boom of thunder and a crackle of lightning to accentuate his tale. Neither happened but when something thumped against the window of the office, I damned near jumped out of my skin.

'What the heck was that?' I asked the air as I put my coffee down and stood up. Before I got moving there was another thump as a second something hit the glass. The sound was like something heavy and solid but also soft like it was made of flesh.

Without questioning whether it was safe to do so, I flung open the door and dashed outside to see who was there.

The street was empty. At almost five o'clock, the Saturday trade of tourists had wound down to almost nothing and the evening crowd of people out for food and drink had yet to arrive. A chill wind blew along the high street carrying the dirty scent of the river at low tide.

I hugged my arms about myself as Frank joined me in the street. 'What was it?' he asked, his eyes darted to take in the two packages on the ground when I nodded my head at them.

I thought he was going to ask what they were, as if I might have any idea, but instead he knelt down next to the nearest of them and gave it a poke. I eyed him nervously, wanting to warn him that it could be a bomb or something even though I didn't believe it likely.

He looked back up before I could say anything. 'I think it's a fish?'

'A fish?'

'Yeah, a fish.' Then from a pocket he produced a butterfly knife and cut the string which held the package shut. As he opened it, I could see it was indeed a fish. A fish that someone had meticulously wrapped in newspaper and thrown at our windows. The other package, lying a few feet further away looked the same. 'There's a message.' Frank said.

I would like to say that I am used to weird goings on but clearly not that used to it because I found this strange. Why would someone throw a fish at the office? Then the stench of the creature hit my nose. 'Oh, my!' I said reeling back to get away from the smell. 'Is that thing going rotten?'

'It's fairly potent,' Frank replied turning his head to one side to take a breath before he opened the package out fully to expose the whole message.' I didn't have to prompt Frank to read it, he did so anyway, 'Stay away from the case or suffer. Does that mean anything to you?'

'What's going on?' asked a voice from behind me, the suddenness and proximity making me almost mess myself.

'Someone threw a rotten fish at Jane's office,' Frank said with a laugh. 'There's a message inside.'

'Of course there is,' replied Poison, flicking her hair to show how cool and casual she was about it. 'I locked up already. See you Monday.'

I murmured a goodbye as Frank bid her a fun Sunday. I had no idea what Poison might do with her time off, but I got the impression she might be some kind of shadow warrior or ninja assassin in her spare time, so I didn't ask.

'You want me to throw this away?' Frank asked.

I shook my head. 'No, it's evidence. This is from whoever is behind the murders at Biddenden Lake. I started looking into it and somehow they know already.' I asked myself what that meant. Who knew about my involvement? A few people at the police station, my grandmother and Jennifer Lasseter. Who among them could have tipped someone off?

Then it hit me: the killer was a member of Kent Police. They had to be. Two police officers had been killed in a copycat of an unsolved crime and if I dismissed my grandmother and Jennifer Lasseter then only the police knew I was involved. I felt the blood drain from my face.

Who should I trust now?

'Um, Frank, just leave them, okay. I'll deal with this.' I wasn't sure how I was going to deal with the stinky fish, but the second package might have a different note in it, and I needed to work fast to find out who was trying to scare me off. As Frank stood up again and put the knife away, I got a sense of how alone and exposed I was without Tempest and Amanda here.

'You're sure?' Frank asked.

I nodded slowly, my mind whirling with all the things I was thinking at once. 'Yes. I've got this.'

Frank didn't look convinced, but he didn't argue. 'Okay. You let me know if you need anything.' I nodded but there was nothing else to say so Frank inclined his head in a quick salute and left me where I was, another breeze of cruel air reminding me that my coat was inside.

Acting fast, I went back inside, grabbed evidence bags from the back store and rushed back outside. I didn't pick up my coat; I was cold but I didn't want it to smell of fish, which I felt convinced was going to happen to everything else I had on.

The fish's dead eyes stared lifelessly back at me as I held my breath and scooped it into a bag. It was leaking all over the note and the newspaper, disgusting fish juice threatening to kill any DNA or fingerprints that might exist. I thought it unlikely I would find anything like that, especially if a trained police officer was behind it, but I was going to preserve as much of the evidence as I could.

With both fish ziplocked into their bags, I finally got back into the warm where I danced my feet around to get some life back into them and looked for somewhere warm to put my hands. Calling Jan to tell him about the fish sounded like the right thing to do, but I already had a full evening planned and what if he was the killer? It was all too much to think about at the moment.

I put the fish in the back store where I prayed the evidence bags would contain the stench, then shut up the office, killed the light and went back out to my car.

All around me and across the city, people were finished with work for the day. They would be settling down to watch movies at home or getting ready to go out on dates or with friends. I had a hastily arranged self-defense class to attend, a stroppy boyfriend to contend with and a night at a stranger's house that might last until morning.

Had I known at that point what the night had in store for me, I would have walked to the nearest bar and stayed there.

Self-defense. Saturday, December 3rd 1800hrs

I HAD NO IDEA where Simon was, but it was a sigh of relief I let out when I discovered he wasn't home. Worried that he might have just popped around the corner and was about to return, I threw what I needed into a bag and left again.

Twenty minutes later, I was feeling nervous and worrying that I looked ridiculous in my sports gear. I wasn't the only guy in the class but there weren't many of us and it was clear it wasn't pitched at young men because all the other attendees were in their sixties. I felt out of place. Not just because of the age difference, though it played a part, mostly it was to do with having to go into the gents changing room in my coat, dress, and boots and then strip off to show the guys I wasn't in the wrong place. Taking my makeup off had drawn a lot of stares and they continued now, the barely concealed elbow nudging inevitably taking place as the women all found out the new guy in the class had shown up in a dress.

'Right everyone, find a place with enough space around you to swing your arms. We are going to perform some warm-up movements.' The man speaking was a six foot something tall beefcake of shaved-skull muscle. He was in his late fifties but looked like he could kick a wall down and then eat it. Despite that, he was softly spoken and encouraging, the effect that of a wise old teacher.

The pace of the class was slow, which, I soon discovered, was because I had mistakenly booked myself into the over fifties class. 'Don't worry about it,' Sensei Dave said. 'It's not a big deal. You get a one on one taster session with me or one of my assistants tonight. If you like it, you get to come back for a class that has students more closely aligned with your ability and age. We like to keep the older students separate because the young ones think they will be slow or weak or something and then end up with a grandmother sitting on their back while they beg for mercy.'

I laughed at that, but his expression let me know he hadn't been joking.

'I'm going to take you through a few basic holds and techniques. That's all we'll have time for tonight, but I think you'll learn a lot just from that. Before we get started, I just want to say that you'll be in close proximity to other people each week. You might want to consider your personal hygiene before turning up next time.'

My face flushed. 'I had a shower this morning. I have a shower every day.'

Sensei Dave sniffed the air. 'You smell like rotten fish, kid. No offense intended. It's not that bad but if you are going to be grappling with people, they will notice.' Then, thankfully moving on, Sensei Dave showed me how to force someone to let go without striking them. Depending on where and how they grabbed you, I could turn their attack to my advantage and pin them in seconds. He brought over Ken, another muscular martial arts master but one who was in his late twenties.

Stepping in close to me, Ken introduced himself and got down into a pose that made him look like a coiled spring. The he stopped. 'Does anyone else smell rotten fish?' he asked. My face coloured again, my embarrassment making it feel like heat was radiating out from my cheeks.

Sensei Dave said something that sounded like Japanese and Ken went back into his crouching pose. Then, using Ken for me to practice on, Sensei Dave let me pin Ken about a hundred times.

Here's the thing about martial arts though: you have to get really, really close to the other person. All the time. I was getting a little sweaty but that wasn't what was going through my mind when Sensei Dave took me onto hip throws. To perform a hip throw I had to turn and shove my bum toward Ken's hip. Only thing is, I kept getting it wrong and bumping up against his junk instead.

And I think he was letting me.

He then confirmed my suspicions when, while lying on the floor for the umpteenth time, he winked at me.

Before I knew it, the session had ended, but there was no doubt that I had enjoyed it. I felt confident, like I could walk into a fight right now and take out twelve guys as if I had been imbued with the power of Bruce Lee during one sixty-minute class. As Sensei Dave reviewed the class and talked about what he had planned for the next one, I decided I had to sign up for more.

Then it was time to go, students and instructors alike all heading for the changing rooms. I knew I would have to go through the rigmarole of putting all my Jane outfit back on and all the makeup and hair that went with it but I wasn't going to do that in front of all the older men that would judge and whisper.

I followed Sensei Dave instead. 'How do I sign up for more classes, please?'

Sensei Dave was putting items into a sports bag and starting to take off his dojo outfit. 'You can do that online. We have classes most nights which cover different aspects of self-defense, including some that specialize in disarming people with knives and guns. Or you can fill out a form right now. Ken can take you through it.'

Sensei Dave nodded his head in the direction of Ken, who had his top off now to reveal his well-developed pecs and washboard abs. He smiled at me in a way that went directly to my groin. An unwelcome but unavoidable reaction was taking place three feet south of my mouth and, as if Ken knew the effect he was having, he chose that moment to drop his trousers.

'You okay, kid?' asked Sensei Dave, seeing me staring brainlessly across the changing room with my mouth open.

I said, 'Mmfffghl,' to demonstrate that I was just fine, then shook my head and walked quickly away before anyone noticed my erection.

'Not that way,' Sensei Dave called after me as I tried to get back into the dojo. 'I locked up already.' I had my back to the room, willing my penis to go back to sleep so I wouldn't scare or freak out all the nice old men who were undoubtedly already staring at me.

Someone tapped me on the arm. 'Whatcha doing?' It was Ken. He was still naked and was also now grinning at me. 'You might want to deal with that,' he said with a quick nod toward my groin. 'I could help if you want to wait for the others to leave. I have a bit in the middle of my back I just can't reach. Maybe... you can wash my back and I'll...' he leaned into whisper the last part, delivering a suggestion that ensured my current trouser problem wasn't going away any time soon.

Knowing what he had done and leaving his words reverberating in my ear, he went for a shower, singing Barbie Girl loud enough for everyone to hear. I thumped my forehead against the gym doors a couple of times and glanced over my shoulder to see if any of the other men in the changing room were leaving yet.

They were. Various shaking heads and looks of disgust being aimed my way as they went. As Sensei Dave picked up his bag, he called out to me, 'You'll need to hurry, kid. Ken will want to lock up soon.' Then he was gone. I needed a shower and the mighty Ken with his meaty tool were in there waiting for me. I was just going to have to stink.

Thankfully, the bulge in my trousers was beginning to subside, but just as I thought I could quickly grab my things and get out, Ken stuck his head around the side of the showers and shouted. 'Are you coming, or what? Put the dress on if you like. I don't mind a bit of kink.'

That sure made my mind up. I ran across the changing room, grabbed all my gear from the locker it was in and legged it.

'Hey, where are you going?' Ken yelled after me, stepping out of the showers to follow. 'Don't be shy. We can pretend you're a girl if you want.' I glanced back and saw my bra on the floor where I had dropped it. I didn't want to go back for it, but those things are expensive. Ken smiled when I turned around, he thought I had changed my mind, but then he too saw the bra and started toward it.

I was much closer, but he started running, building up speed as he came. I snagged the fallen garment and darted back toward the door squealing in fright as I ducked through it and back outside. Then Ken slammed into the doors, the sound making me think he had slipped and the cussing that followed confirmed it.

I hurried away and got to my car. I was going to have to go home to shower and change and run the gauntlet of seeing Simon once again.

My First Stakeout. Saturday, December 3rd 2018hrs

As AGREED, I CALLED Karen from my car to let her know I was on my way and would be arriving soon. The satnav claimed I had five minutes left of my drive to her house but my plan to sneak in around the back would add at least another five minutes to the time. I told her that and asked her to sit tight by the back door. She wasn't happy about being in the house by herself but she agreed to it, reluctantly telling me she was on her way to the house now.

Earlier today, she showed me an alleyway that ran between the houses. From it, I could jump a couple of low fences to gain access to her garden. I scoped out as much before I left this afternoon so my confidence in this element of the task was high.

Simon still wasn't home when I got there an hour ago, but he had left a note which was sweet of him. It read, 'Sorry I have been grumpy. I had a tough week and wanted to spend some time having fun with you. Let's make it up to each other tomorrow.' There was also a small bunch of flowers with the note, bright pink gerberas which he knew were my favourite.

Buoyed by his *sort of* apology, I took my time scrubbing the dead fish smell from my hands and hair and everywhere else. I hadn't touched the fish with my bare skin but close proximity to it seemed to be enough for the smell to transfer. Not that I could smell it but if Ken and Sensei Dave were anything to go by, it was clear the stench had stayed with me.

From my wardrobe I selected kick-ass, vampire-killer boots with laces all the way up the outsides, They were such a very dark burgundy they almost looked black and I paired them with black leggings and a little black dress that flared at the waist to ensure I could move my legs freely if I needed to run away or, heaven forbid, protect Karen and myself from the Sandman. Makeup, my blonde wig and a large black handbag in the crook of my right arm. A quick check in the mirror told me I was ready to go and looked good.

Now, sitting in a dark spot on the street, parked well away from any streetlights, I felt anything but ready. This no longer felt like a good idea. What if the Sandman did show up? I should have left this case for Tempest. I bit my lip. I was letting nervousness manifest as indecision. To be an investigator, I would have to be tougher than this. Able to walk into any situation and take charge. That was how I needed to be.

I swore at myself in the quiet of my car, shoved the door open with a reluctant shoulder and got out. Just along the road I could see the gap in the garden walls that marked the entrance to the alleyway. It looked different in the dark but I reminded myself that all I had to do was jump a couple of low fences and I would be there. Once inside Karen's house, I could relax. There was very little likelihood the Sandman would show up tonight. He had never come two nights in a row before. Most likely he was off bothering someone else.

That thought made me pause though. What if I was right? What if the reason he hadn't been to Karen's house two nights in a row was because he was doing the same thing to multiple people? Paused at the entrance to the alleyways while I pondered that thought, I felt suddenly exposed. Looking about to see if anyone was watching, I hurried down the path and let the blackness envelope me.

Karen's house was three doors along, so I had to climb over three fences to get to her back garden. The first one felt sturdy enough and was only three feet high, so I placed my hands on top of it and vaulted over. Landing nimbly the other side, I felt my confidence growing again. The next fence was much the same though I had to pick a spot because there were lots of rose bushes on the other side. The fence into Karen's garden was higher though; four feet instead of three which I wasn't sure I could just vault over. I could get over it, sure, but I wanted to do so quietly and without snagging my leggings. Looking about, I found a garden chair and dragged it to where the fence was clear of plants on both sides. With the chair up against the fence for added stability, I climbed onto it and then much the same as before I placed my hands on top of the wood and drove myself upwards to vault over.

The fence collapsed.

The two previous times on approaching the fence, I gave it a quick if gentle rattle to check how sturdy it was. The overlapping pine fence panels were notoriously weak, but people bought them because they were cheap. In the dark I couldn't see it, but this one was rotting and falling apart. My weight had been far too much additional responsibility for it to bear.

The wood splintering as I crashed to the ground on top of it made a deafening racket but as I lay stunned and winded on the lawn, no faces appeared at any windows, including Karen's.

There were lights on inside her house but no sign of her. I guess she had been looking out for me, seen me approaching and got to turn the TV on or something. I stole quietly up to her back door and let myself in.

I couldn't go further into her house because it was carpeted beyond the kitchen tiles and I had muddy boots from the alleyway and the garden, plus bits of grass on my knees and elbows from my tumble. I placed my handbag on the kitchen counter so I could unzip a boot but when someone came into the room, it wasn't Karen's feet I saw through my fringe as it hung over my eyes, but a pair of man's shoes.

The Sandman was already in the house!

The jolt of adrenalin sent my pulse skyrocketing, but I came back upright ready to fight. He was reaching for me, his right hand extended forward, so I grabbed it just the way that Sensei Dave showed me with Ken.

The man was somewhere around sixty, with thinning hair and a bloodshot face. His nose was pointed, with a large hooked bridge and a weak jaw. He looked like someone that would cut off a person's skin and wear it around the house as a coat.

Driven by terror, I yanked him off balance before he could even say a word, twisting his hand around so the wrist went beyond its natural stopping point.

He yelped in pain and protested, 'What are you doing?' I had the upper hand and I wasn't about to let it go. I couldn't see a weapon but that didn't mean he didn't have one, and what about the drugs he was using to knock her out each time? They had to be on him somewhere. As I applied yet more pressure to his arm and forced him to turn away from me, I swung a kick at the back of his right knee and down he went.

Now I had him. Yay! Go team Jane!

Drawn by the ruckus, Karen screeched to a stop in the kitchen doorway. 'Oh, my life! What's happening?'

'Quick. Call the police. I've got him.' I couldn't resist the smile that forced its way onto my face. Wait until I tell Tempest about this.

Karen grabbed my arm. 'That's my neighbor, Mr Hengist.'

Oops.

Not wanting to let go yet, I asked, 'You're sure? You're sure this isn't the Sandman? Couldn't he be the Sandman?'

'No,' she cried, flapping her arms for me to stop hurting the man and let him go. 'He just brought a parcel around that got delivered this morning. He helped me carry it in.'

'Oh.' I let go of his wrist. 'Um, sorry about that.'

Mr Hengist stood up, rubbing his wrist and rolling his shoulder to ease off the strain I had put it under. 'Where do you get your friends, Karen? This one is a bit nuts.'

'Sorry,' I said again. 'I thought you were here to hurt Karen.'

73

'Why on earth would I hurt Karen? You know what; nevermind. Karen, I'm going home. Thank you, it was lovely, I'll let myself out.' Still shaking off his arm, Karen's neighbor walked to the front door and slammed it shut behind him.

Karen and I exchanged an embarrassed glance. 'Oops,' she said. 'That was quite impressive though. You weren't kidding about being a ninja, were you?'

'Ah, no,' I lied

Karen went around me to make sure the back door was closed, then locked it and threw a bolt at the top and the bottom. 'That's got me all on edge. Let's go watch some TV, yes?'

In her living space, Karen sat down next to a large glass of wine and I could tell from the condensation line that she had taken a big gulp out of it already. 'You said you don't want any?' she confirmed. I actually did but I said no anyway. The encounter with her neighbor had me rattled even though it had gone my way. I was certain though that were I to have a glass, I would want another and drinking while on a stakeout couldn't be a clever move. Neither of the other detectives at the firm would entertain the idea, so I didn't either.

Within a few minutes I had installed the cameras in her bedroom and checked they worked; the feed to my laptop was clear and crisp, and I was back downstairs on Karen's couch wondering what I should do next. I wasn't sure what I had expected from my first stakeout, but it certainly wasn't what I got. For months now, living with Simon, we went out on a Saturday night, so I hadn't watched weekend TV for ages. Over the next two hours of the evening, Karen and I burned through a game show and a live TV singing contest where we got to say unkind things about the fools who had volunteered to go on stage to show the world they couldn't hold a note.

It was fun. Probably more fun than I would have had out with Simon and his friends. I say his friends because they were all people that he worked with or knew from school or something. I was friendly with them and they were pleasant enough to me, but none of them ever made separate plans with me; they were very much Simon's friends.

At ten thirty, when the singing show finished, Karen yawned and stretched and told me she was going to bed. Her bottle of wine was long gone, as were the two gin and tonics she made to wash the wine down with. I was going to stay on the couch. It was close to the door out of the small living room which was directly opposite the stairs. From the couch, no one could get to the stairs without first having to get by me. I didn't think it was all that much in terms of security but Karen said she felt safe enough to get some sleep so that was where she was heading. She asked me to be with her when she unlocked the backdoor to call for her cat to come in for the night and seemed relieved when he appeared.

We each said a polite goodnight and I flicked the lights off once she was upstairs. Now drenched in darkness, I wondered how long I could or should stay awake.

The answer was not very long at all as my eyes soon got heavy and I didn't bother to fight it.

All too soon though, I came awake and was instantly gripped by utter panic.

Fire. Sunday, December 4th OO48hrs

THE PIERCING NOISE OF a smoke alarm took me from deep slumber to instantly disorientated panic in half a second. There has to be a primordial instinct still wired into all of us because the fear of fire is right up there on my list of top ten worst ways to die.

Coming awake had caused me to sit up but as smoke filled my lungs, I started coughing. From upstairs came an equally panicked shout as Karen also began coughing. I could hear her feet on the floorboards above as she started toward the stairs.

Slowly, my sleep addled brain came online, and I remembered what I was supposed to do: get low. I threw myself off the couch, landing on my handbag which I gratefully hooked an arm through. There was a thin pocket of air right by the carpet and though it was dark, I knew the way out. Smoke filled the air above me, glowing orange with the fire though I could not tell which direction it was coming from until I got out of the living room and into the hallway.

By then, Karen was coming down the stairs, coughing great racking lungfuls of smoke as she fought to get out of the house and away from danger. I grabbed her ankle when a foot appeared next to me, her scream of terror shut off as she coughed again. Doing what I felt necessary, I grabbed her other foot and yanked them both so she landed on the floor next to me.

I screamed in her face, 'Front door!' then pushed her in the direction she needed to go. No more words were needed, but one of us had to stand up to open the door when we got there. Karen was barely able to stop coughing at all so took a last desperate lungful of the slightly less smoky air and stood up. I knew from a health and safety video I had once been forced to watch that a lungful of hot air will destroy your lungs instantly and that in a household fire, the temperature can be expected to reach over one thousand degrees in a matter of seconds. Whatever else I did, I couldn't afford to take a breath.

Keeping my eyes shut, I found the safety catch and yanked the door open. Merciful light spilled in from outside along with blessed cold air, but the door caught on something unseen. Was it Karen? I gave it another yank with the same result. The heat behind us was building, but we couldn't escape even though I could sense sanctuary mere feet away.

'The chain,' coughed Karen from by my feet. 'The chain!'

Of course. She had a safety chain on the front door. I still had my eyes shut and no intention of opening them. Instead, I braced myself, pushed the door shut a few inches and yanked with all my might. To my surprise the chain broke, ripping free of its mooring point on the frame and the door flew open.

Cold air billowed in just as smoke billowed out, the two intertwining and dancing like sparring partners looking for an opening. I tumbled onto the front lawn with my bag and looked around to find Karen right behind me. We were out.

'Mr Bagatus,' Karen wheezed. It took her three attempts to say his name between coughing fits but if the cat was inside, I didn't fancy his chances. I couldn't go back in to look for him. But as I worried for the cat, he appeared, strolling along to waft his tail under Karen's nose. She scooped him up.

Sirens, which I realised I had been able to hear from inside the house got really loud as they pulled into the street, their flashing lights bouncing off every surface. Suddenly boots were running down the garden path as a flurry of activity happened all at once. Firefighters came to tend to us both, soothing voices assuring us that the paramedics were right behind them and there were insistent questions about who else was in the house.

The blaze was out in a minute, but Karen's house was not fit to be lived in anymore and the repairs would take weeks or months. 'Karen, I'm so sorry,' I said as we sat in the back of an ambulance. The paramedics had us both hooked up to oxygen and were monitoring our vital signs.

She waved me to silence. 'You didn't set the fire, Jane. He did.'

'He who?' asked the paramedic as he checked her blood/oxygen level again. 'Did someone start this fire deliberately?'

Karen and I looked at each other. We couldn't prove it but we both believed the Sandman had turned to arson. Maybe it was because he knew I was there, maybe it was something else that triggered it, but there was too much coincidence for either of us to believe this was just an unfortunate accident.

A firefighter came to the back of the ambulance. His uniform displayed his rank as did his helmet so I knew he was the crew chief. 'How's everyone doing? Are you ladies okay?' I nodded and Karen gave him a thumbs up. I wasn't sure she meant it. His face turned serious then as he delivered the next bit of news. 'The fire was started deliberately. Someone put paraffin under the back door and lit it. The police will want to talk to you. Any idea who might want to do this?'

I nodded again. 'Yes, but at this time the likely perpetrator is an unknown person. A stalker if you will.'

My comment got raised eyebrows from the fire chief. 'Well, the police will want to talk to you.' He repeated.

As he made to move away, I stopped him with a question, 'How did you get here so quickly?' He turned back to face me. 'We had barely had time to register that there was a fire and get out. The fire couldn't have been going for more than a couple of minutes before you arrived.'

'Yeah, we weren't called for a house fire. Someone set fire to a car down the street. The resident that reported it put it out with a couple of fire extinguishers before it really got going, but called us and... well, you can't be too careful when you have a car fire because of all the combustibles.'

A worry itched at the top of my scalp. 'What sort of car was it, please?'

His eyes went to the top of his skull as he searched his memory for the answer. 'A little Ford Fiesta, I think.'

Dammit. 'Was it a green one?'

Grimly, he said, 'Can't tell now. It was a dark colour once. Now it's just burnt.'

Dammit. The Sandman had torched my car too. I pulled off the oxygen mask and levered myself off the gurney. I needed to see for myself. I was right though; my car was toast. I did a mental tot up of what was in it, trying to work out if I had any of my favourite outfits in there, but all I could come up with was a few CDs. Tears threatened; I was having a tough couple of days.

I sensed someone approaching and turned to find a female police officer approaching with a male colleague trailing just a few feet behind. 'Is this your car, Miss?' she asked. I nodded glumly. 'And you were in the house that suffered the arson attack?'

I nodded again, fixing my face with a wobbly smile as I looked up her. 'Yeah. I'm not having a good day.'

'I should say not,' the officer agreed as she held out an arm to guide me back down the street. 'I think we should get you back to the ambulance, I don't think they were finished with you. Then I need to get some basic details.'

I complied. I had no reason not to, but I should have thought about what was going to happen because once I was back at the ambulance, and was sitting next to Karen once more, the cop asked me for my identification.

'Um, can we do this later?' I tried.

She eyed me suspiciously. 'Why?'

I opened my mouth to argue or to try to move the conversation somewhere else, but I saw the futility of it. Feeling everyone's eyes on me, I took out my purse, slid the driver's license from its slot and handed it over. She took it and handed it to her colleague so she had both hands free to write in her notebook.

When he didn't start speaking, she turned to stare at him. He was looking at me and looking at the card. 'This isn't you,' he said, squinting at me like they had just identified something very fishy going on.

He showed the female cop and I saw her eyes open wider just before she swung her gaze back to stare at me. Karen was looking at me too now. Reluctantly, and with a lump in my throat, I reached up to my head, pulled out the pin that held my wig in place and took it off.

'It's me,' I admitted. I did so in my own voice and didn't have to spare a glance at Karen to know that her face with filled with revulsion. I shifted my head ever so slightly towards her when I said, 'Sorry,' but I kept my eyes down.

Just then, a taxi nosed into the street. I spotted it but gave it no thought until it stopped just behind the nearest police car and Simon got out. I texted him when the fire was being fought, asking him if he was having a nice evening and just dropping in conversationally that the house I was in had been fire-bombed so I would be home soon and might need a hug.

Now he was here, coming to rescue me and boy did I feel like I needed him. He got stopped at the perimeter by a cop stationed there to do just that, neighbours had spilled from their houses, many of them with kids, just to watch the spectacle and they lined the hastily erected barrier tape, but when Simon pointed and explained who he was trying to get to, the cops let him through.

With a tear in my eye, I raised my hand to wave, but it faltered halfway up when I saw his face. It had thunderous murder etched into it. Seeing him approach, the male cop leaned forward to speak to his female colleague. He didn't bother to whisper though when he said, 'Look out; trouble coming.'

She turned, but Simon was already starting to speak. 'What the heck have you got yourself into this time?'

'I.'

'I told you to steer clear of this paranormal nonsense. I told you not to apply for the job in the first place and now someone has targeted you and this... this poor woman. I take it that was your house that just got burned down?' he asked Karen.

'I,' I tried again but he just steamrollered on.

Or rather he didn't. I started speaking and stopped because he was looking at Karen and then looking at me and then his hand went to his mouth. 'Oh, my goodness,' he sucked in a huge shocked breath. 'This is why you've been avoiding me. Isn't it? You've gone back to women, haven't you?'

The male cop handed my driver's license back to the female cop as he said, 'I'm out. This is way too new world weird for me.'

Simon snarled at me with gritted teeth, 'I want you out. I want you out tonight. Your things will be waiting for you in the garage when you get there.' Then, before I could protest or argue, he spun on a heel and stormed off.

It was silent in the back of the ambulance for a few seconds and as time stretched out and no one said anything, I got angry. Angry at how I felt now. So much had happened that I should have been able to control, but I hadn't. I let it happen and Simon dumping me felt like the last straw. I looked around at all the faces staring at me.

'Yes, I'm a guy, okay?' I snapped in my normal voice.

Karen said, 'Ewww.'

Then the paramedic leaned across to reattach the blood/oxygen monitor and I slapped it away. Ignoring his cry of protest, I shuffled my backside off the gurney and back onto the pavement.

'Hold on,' said the cop. She looked like she had seen it all before or heard it all before and was just too bored to be surprised by it. 'I still need to get a statement from you.' Then she saw the desperate look in my eyes and let her shoulders slump in defeat. 'We can do it over there out of everyone's way.'

She pointed to spot on the pavement a few feet away. It wasn't private, but it was far enough for me to feel like I wasn't being watched by everyone. We didn't get there though. A shout that rang above the sound of everything else going on, stopped us both short.

'Hey tranny, what's going on with your hair?' I turned to see Police Constable Patience Woods approaching me at speed, her ample hips swinging as she came. I knew her through Amanda. The two women had been beat cops together until quite recently when Amanda quit and took the job at Blue Moon. Patience had a way with words that was just plain offensive, but she always seemed genuinely pleased to see me. 'I got it from here, sugar,' she shouted. The cop with me raised a hand to show she was fine with handing me over and walked away.

Then Patience arrived, finally catching up to where her presence had been felt several seconds earlier. She was like that; her personality a whole lot bigger than the woman it was stuck inside. 'Hey girl,' she said, offering me a high five. I glanced beyond her to where I could see a more senior officer frowning in her direction. 'You should fix your hair, sugar. You don't look right without it.'

I mumbled my thanks and used the light shining on a nearby car window to get it straight. When I had it in place, Patience said, 'You look like crap, girl. Why don't you tell me what's been going on and how you come to be in a house that's on fire.'

So, I told her all about Tempest and Amanda being away, to which she asked, 'Do you think those two are finally hooking up? I swear, at the speed they were moving, I thought I was gonna have to grease up his thing and push him into her.'

I snorted at that point, finally finding something funny in the chaos around me. I had no car, I had nowhere to live and I had no boyfriend it seemed. Patience made me laugh though, not just then, but several more times as I told her about the Sandman and how I was trying to be an investigator too.

She took my statement, in her usual half-assed kind of way and confirmed I was free to go. Go where though? That was what I had to ask myself. I could collect my things from Simon's place tomorrow or whatever, but it was cold out tonight despite the heavy blanket the firefighters gave me, and I had nowhere to go and no way to get there. I could ask gran if I could move back in. I knew she would say yes, but I wasn't going to wake her in the middle of the night, hammering on her door to be let in.

Forlornly, I looked at my car keys and clicked the plipper thing to open it. When the lights flashed to announce it was unlocked, I sobbed a little laugh that it still worked, but then I spotted my solution for the night. I still had a key to Tempest's house on my keyring. It was right there, hanging from the bunch with all the others. He had given me the keyring a few weeks ago when his office burned down and he wanted me to work from the office in his house until he could get a new place.

He wasn't there and I was certain he wouldn't mind. I still felt uncomfortable about just letting myself in without his permission though, so I sent him a text message to say I needed a place to stay and was going to crash on his couch until the morning and hoped that was okay. It was close to three in the morning in France which meant he most likely wouldn't read the message until after I had stayed the night, but as I looked around to see if there was any chance I could get a lift back into Maidstone, my phone pinged and his reply was there on the screen: I should sleep in the spare room and stay as long as I needed.

At least something was going right for me, but as I stared sleepily out the back window of Patience's squad car as we swept along the country lanes, I couldn't help but wonder who the Sandman was and how he had known about me. Was the house bugged? Was he watching from across the street? Whoever he was, he had known enough to target my car.

Patience was good enough to drop me off in Finchampstead right outside Tempest's house. I thanked her and said goodnight then stumbled into the house, grabbed a shower because I stank of smoke and my face and hands were filthy and finally, at close to four in the morning, I sank into cool, crisp sheets and fell instantly asleep.

The sound of a man quietly singing Mr Sandman woke me up.

Tempest's House.
Sunday, December 4th
O447hrs

I SAT BOLT UPRIGHT in bed, drenched in nervous sweat and breathing hard from the shock of his voice only to find myself alone. I clutched at my chest, my heart still racing from the vivid dream. I slept fitfully after that, eventually winning the fight for sleep sometime around six and sleeping right through until almost ten when the sound of my phone ringing woke me.

Coming awake, I looked around for it, found myself hopelessly disorientated until I remembered where I was and then still couldn't find it or my handbag until after it had rung off. As it switched to voicemail, I found it along with last night's clothes tucked in a pile at the foot of the bed. The caller was Tempest but he hadn't left a message so the phone reset itself to standby mode as I picked it up.

I called him back. 'Hi, Tempest. How are things in France?'

Tempest sounded like he was in a great mood when he started talking. 'It's beautiful here. Amanda and I are going to have one more day on the slopes and head home tonight. We should be in the office tomorrow morning as usual. How are things back there? Did I understand correctly that you have split up with Simon?'

I scratched my head as I wondered how to answer. He was having a great time and hopefully was now involved with Amanda so there was no good reason to tell him all about how awful my last twelve hours had been. I gave him the skinny version. 'My car got kind of destroyed and yes I split up with Simon. I just needed a place for the night though. I'll be moving in with gran again today. Thank you so much for letting me crash here last night.'

'Hey, no problem. I'm glad you had a key. What happened to your car though?'

'Oh, um, well, with you both away, I decided to look into another case. Chief Inspector Quinn hired us actually,' I admitted carefully, unsure what Tempest's reaction might be.

'Really?' he asked, sounding utterly unbothered. 'Well, that's new. What's the case?'

This was so typical for Tempest. Hear the news, process and move on. I told him about the drowning that wasn't a drowning and about the swamp monster and the two new murders and Jan Van Doorn although I left out the bit about Jan having a delicious-looking bum.

When I finished, he said, 'Well, you don't have to do anything, but if you feel like pursuing this, please do so carefully. With us away you have no back up. Oh, and you should take my car until I get back. We'll have to sort you out some new wheels early next week. It's no good you being immobile and trying to walk to work or get the bus. Don't go doing anything daft like getting a loan either, I clearly owe you extra pay for solving cases you haven't been telling me about. We can discuss it when I get back. The keys are in the utility room next to the front door.'

I wasn't sure I had heard him right. 'You want me to take your car until you get back?'

'Yes,' he replied as if unsure why I would be seeking conformation.

'Your Porsche?'

'Yes.'

'Righto. Just wanted to check.'

'It's just a car, Jane. Have fun with it though.' We disconnected the call and I leapt from bed to look out the window at his car. Tempest drove a bright red Porsche Boxster S with a full factory-fitted body kit and huge wheels. It looked fantastic, especially when compared to my little Ford Fiesta. The Porsche wasn't new, but it wasn't exactly old either and I knew he kept it in immaculate condition.

Any thoughts of moping about were gone. I had a car to drive and I was going to do just that.

There was no milk in the house, so I took my coffee black and strong. I was tired but the buzz from the caffeine soon had me moving. I had a whole list of things I needed to do, such as speak with gran and confirm I could move in with her, collect my things from Simon's, and get some serious research done into the Sandman and the swamp monster cases. So far, I had been in possession of the swamp monster case file for twenty-four hours but had barely looked at it. That was unlike me; I was the research genius.

Clothes were a big problem too. What I had on yesterday was trashed, or at least far too stinky from smoke to consider putting back on. I looked in Tempest's wardrobe for some old bits I might borrow but all his clothes were simply too big for me to wear though I did borrow a hoody to go over my sweaty sports gear which I reluctantly put back on because it was the only option I had.

First things first, boot up the computer in Tempest's office and do some research. I wanted to build up a background picture for each case, so I started with the Sandman as I was convinced he was the one that tried to kill me last night. At the office, I ran a set up with three screens which made opening files and moving information about very easy. Using a single screen felt like I was trying to do it on a blackboard or something, so I switched to making notes on my tablet by hand.

There were no entries anywhere for the Sandman; he just didn't exist. I wasn't looking for a person called the Sandman, of course, but for references to a person that appeared in people's houses at night and sang to them. There were supernatural press sites and other places to look but I got no hits at all. It was perplexing. You might wonder why I was still throwing my time and effort at the case given Karen's attitude last night, but she hadn't actually released me from the investigation so my plan was to do what I could and hand it over for Tempest to continue on his return.

Just when I was ready to give up and start looking at the swamp monster case instead, I decided to perform a search for the Sandman after all. Using the search term *sung to sleep by a spooky sandman*, I got a hit.

It was two years old and posted by a woman named River Tam. It was on a forum for people suffering recurring nightmares and there was a lot of conversation that followed her starter topic. I read it all, which took a while, but it was all the same thing. In her first post she claimed she suffered vivid dreams in which a man was sitting in her bedroom singing Mr Sandman to her. This was it! This was evidence that the man plaguing Karen Gilbert had done it before.

People responding to her post gave her remedies and coping techniques to stop the dreams recurring and how to manage the night terrors when they occurred. Two replies later, she told the group she no longer believed they were dreams and that someone was coming into her house. The responses then were mixed. Most people were supportive but didn't believe her, some were just plain cruel and told her to stop being dramatic: they're just dreams.

She wrote three more posts. In each she grew more convinced that she was being targeted by a man. After that, all the posts were from other people.

I opened a new search and looked for her specifically. She was easy to find because her username on the recurring dream forum was her name, whereas most people used something else like Dreamless123 or Krugersafterme22.

Though finding her wasn't a problem, where I found her was: She was in the obituaries. There was a picture and a few sentences. The blurb of her obituary didn't tell me anything useful, but my jaw fell open when I took a second look at her picture: it could have been Karen Gilbert. They looked so similar it couldn't be a coincidence. Forcing myself to move on, I opened yet another search, this time looking for a police report or newspaper article that would tell me something pertinent.

I found it soon enough. River Tam disappeared from her home one night and was found by a farmer eight days later. She was in a field and arranged as if asleep with a blanket over her and a pillow under her head.

I snatched up my phone and called the number for Karen. It rang a few times, long enough for her to see whose number it was and then the line came up busy. I tried again, this time getting the busy signal almost immediately: she was rejecting the call. I would have to go there.

Go where though? Where was she staying? I had no idea. I didn't even have an email from her to which I could send a message because she had walked in off the street. I could send a text though so that was what I did. Skipping any apology for deceiving her over my gender, I told her the Sandman had struck before and she might be in more danger than we realized. I ended it with a plea that she call me.

Further research to find other victims got me nowhere but time was ticking on and I really had to deal with other things. That I couldn't reach Karen was scaring me; she didn't know how much danger she might be in. Tapping my phone on my chin as I tried to work the problem in my head, I grasped what felt like my only option and called Jan.

He picked up straight away. 'Hello. Is that you, Jane? Are you okay?'

'Um, yeah. Why do you ask?' His voice was filled with concern as if I might not be okay at all.

'Weren't you in a house fire last night. Patience told me all about it. I didn't know that you two knew each other.'

Oh yeah: the fire. 'Yes, thank you for asking. I'm fine. My clothes stink and my car got burnt out, but otherwise there's nothing wrong with me. I called to ask you a question actually.' I skipped over how I knew Patience because it wasn't important and because it would give me something to use as a conversation starter later.

I heard him grab a pen and click it. 'Go on.'

'The house I was in was that of a client. I am emailing you some screen shots and documents right now. You remember I told you about a guy breaking into a woman's house to sing her a song? Well, that's my client and he is using some kind of incapacitant on her.'

'An incapacitant?' he interrupted. 'Like a date rape drug?'

'Possibly. I haven't got very far with that yet and she hasn't had an incident since she approached the firm so I couldn't get her blood checked even if I wanted to.'

He sighed quietly at the other end. 'That most likely wouldn't show anything anyway. Date rape drugs like Rohypnol are basically benzodiazepine, a drug originally designed as a pre-anesthetic. The metabolites in it leave the body immediately so the only way to find trace amounts is through a urine sample but that has to be collected swiftly after the attack and rarely is because the drug causes amnesia, disorientation and confusion. They have got so developed now that they are almost always untraceable by the time the victim is alert enough to report the crime. Is he assaulting her?'

I shook my head even though he couldn't see it. 'No, so far there is no sign that he has even touched her. Check the second file I sent though.' I waited for him to get it open.

'The body in the field?' he asked.

'Yes. River Tam, the victim in the picture, reported the exact same MO before she vanished and was later found dead. The stalker breaks into their house and sings Mr Sandman to them while they are drugged. River Tam might be the only murder victim but there could be more. The ritual she reports is too close to my client's for it to be coincidence and see how she is arranged in the field? It looks loving. He sings them to sleep, kills them and then arranges them delicately. But something changed last night and it might have been my presence at the house. I don't know who he is or how he might have connected me, but I go to her house and the next thing I know my car is burnt out and her house is on fire. Now my client won't answer my calls and I don't know where she is and I think she might be in extreme danger.'

'You want me to help track her down?' he asked, already knowing the answer.

'I'm going to go at it from my end too, but I think we have to contact her friends and family and find out where she is.' I felt relieved to have some help finally.

'Okay. I'm on it. I'll let you know what I find.'

He sounded like he was going to end the call, so I jumped in again quickly. 'Jan, about the other case?'

'You mean the swamp monster?'

'Yeah, that one. What do you think about setting a trap to lure the killer out? I discovered that both the victims were on Meet Market, the online dating agency...'

'The one with the unofficial slogan, "Who wants a bite of my meat?" Really classy site that one.'

'That's the one. Well, they were both using it. I'm playing a big hunch here but if they were deliberately targeted, it seems like a good way to lure the killer out. I can create a fake profile and claim to be a police officer, use a couple of library shots and photo-processing to superimpose my face, that sort of thing. What do you think?'

'Um, well I see two major flaws.' I hadn't expected this. He was being instantly negative. 'Firstly, you're a girl. And secondly, you're a girl. I realise that technically this is the same point repeated, but it seems like such a big point that it warrants saying twice.'

I hadn't thought about that. In my head I was just going to use a picture of me as James, but Jan only knew me as Jane. Rather than explain I just said, 'I hadn't thought of that.'

'I can't do it either, I'm afraid. The chief inspector would never endorse it.' I nodded mutely and tried to rethink how to approach the issue. I would just upload my fake profile as intended and see if I could get a date. It was a simple enough thing to do; I would largely copy the profiles of the two murdered men in the hope there was something generic about them that attracted the killer.

'Jane, how was it you managed to find out about their Meet Market profiles? Isn't all that stuff encrypted?'

'Sorry, someone at the door, got to go.' I quickly ended the call. I had basically told him I was hacking people's social media accounts because I am dumb and forgot he is a cop.

Thinking it unlikely I had heard the last of that conversation, I called my gran, a task I put off earlier because I knew she would have hobbled to church this morning and would not get home until almost noon. My stomach growled at me while I waited for the call to connect. There was no fresh produce in Tempest's house, not even fruit and I hadn't bothered to raid his cupboards though I was sure I would have found something had I done so. Getting higher on my list of things to do was get something to eat.

'Hello,' gran's wobbly voice came on the line.

'Hi, gran. It's James.' I used my real name because I was wearing boy clothes and that felt right.

I got a tut in response. 'You really should pick one name and stick with it. I get so confused working out what to call you.'

'Okay, gran,' I replied, trying to move the conversation along. 'You said yesterday that you missed having me around and I could move back in if I wanted to...' I left that hanging to let it sink in.

After a pause, she said, 'No. No, I don't remember saying that.'

'Oh. Well you did.' This was difficult. Where was I going to stay if I couldn't move back in with gran. More importantly perhaps was the concern that my gran couldn't remember our conversation from yesterday; she was eighty-four, but was this dementia showing itself?'

'Only joking,' she laughed. 'Everyone expects me to be losing my marbles just because I'm getting on a bit. I did the crossword in twelve minutes yesterday. When should I expect you?'

Breathing a sigh of relief both for myself and for her, I performed a quick mental calculation. 'In a couple of hours? I need to collect my things, but I will arrive mid-afternoon I suppose. Is that okay?'

'Will you want dinner? Only, I took out a dinner for myself and have nothing for you.'

'That's okay, gran. I'll feed myself.' If all I had to worry about was what to feed myself, I had nothing to worry about at all. I would grab a burger and fries somewhere.

I thanked her and disconnected. Right, now that I had a place to stay, I needed to put my brave pants on and face Simon. It would be painful and awkward, but it would be over soon. Karen still hadn't responded to my text, so with nothing else I could use as an excuse to put it off, I gathered my things, made sure Tempest's house was left tidy, and went to the door.

Then, as I opened the door and looked outside, I remembered that my car was destroyed, and I had to drive the Porsche instead.

Let's just say I got to Simon's faster than expected.

Break ups. Sunday, December 4th 1303hrs

CLAIMING I GOT TO Simon's place fast was a little misleading because I took my time and stopped for burgers on the way there. The bits when I was driving though, well, at those points I was moving fast. Faster than I should have been probably and the Porsche was so low to the road that it felt even faster.

Taking the corner into his place in West Farleigh, I was still going too fast and the gravel driveway offered very little traction for the car's fat wheels. A slew of gravel sprayed out as the wheels span, pebbles striking Simon's Audi and setting off the alarm.

Unperturbed, and wearing a forced smile, I swung out of the car just as Simon burst from his front door to see what was happening outside.

'Jane? I mean James?' he said, taking in that I was actually dressed in boy clothes for once.

'Yes. You wanted me to collect my things so here I am.' A face appeared behind Simon, one of his friends who I had always suspected was interested in being a little more than a friend. Well, good luck to them I told myself.

'But, but, whose car is that?' Simon stuttered.

'Are my things in the garage?' I demanded. I had no intention of answering his questions.

He looked taken aback, but his friend was nudging him to act or say something. As I strode toward them, looking ridiculous in my oversize hoody and ill-matching sportswear, Simon blinked a couple of times and found his voice. 'Um, no. I hadn't gotten around to it yet.'

I didn't break stride as I reached the house either, walking straight by both of them as I let myself in. 'Not to worry, I'll do it myself.'

'Tell him he can't come in, Simon,' protested his friend. I was already in though, heading to the bedroom where most of my clothing was located. I didn't have much to collect; a few books, some CDs, a small television and a stack of IT gear. Everything else was clothing. It would be a squeeze to get it all in the Porsche but I wasn't doing two trips.

In the bedroom, my feet stopped moving as I took in the two coffee mugs, one on each bedside table. I was pretty sure it meant someone had made coffee and brought it back to bed for the pair of them. I had been sleeping in that bed until yesterday.

Angry that he had replaced me so quickly and easily, I started moving again and had to curb my natural urge to rip my clothes from their hangers. Taking a few deep breaths, I took the hangers as well. Then, as I grabbed the first armful, I caught sight of myself in the mirror. I looked a state. Even as James, who is far less attractive than Jane, I still looked awful. I hadn't slept well and had bags under my eyes, but it was the outfit that bothered me more than anything.

I put my armful of clothes down on the bed, thought about what I wanted to wear and started changing. My night-out wig came out of its hiding place. It cost a small fortune so only got rare use and I kept it on a dummy head at the back of the wardrobe with a protective cover over it. The hair on it was platinum blonde with fine pink highlights. It was overkill for today but my wig from last night needed to be professionally cleaned to get rid of the smoke smell and my transformation into Jane required the hair more than anything else.

Twenty minutes later, the fastest I have ever done it, and with Simon's friend getting audibly impatient outside, I gave myself one final check in the dressing table mirror and stood up. Now I was ready to pack my things and leave.

Simon remained silent throughout, standing in the open plan kitchen area watching me as I took bits out to the car and came back in again. When all the clothes and shoes and bags and accessories and makeup and paraphernalia were out of the bedroom, I knelt on the carpet by the CD collection and started pulling out those that were mine. I only had a few because the world had gone digital and everything was on my phone now. They held some nostalgic value though, so I took them and standing back up, I glanced around, checking mentally to see if there was anything else I could reasonably claim was mine. When I couldn't come up with anything significant, I walked wordlessly out of the house, slid into the car and made sure I gunned the engine to send a fresh spray of gravel.

As I pulled into the street, the alarm on his car was going off once more and he appeared in my rearview, running across to inspect for damage.

It had been my first properly gay relationship and Simon could be labelled perhaps as my first love. Somehow, even though I was now tearing up, I had held my head high and maintained my composure as I moved myself out of his life.

I didn't want to focus my efforts or thoughts on what had been. I had a life ahead of me; there would be other boys, but right now I had two cases on the go and that had to be exciting, right?

If only I knew how wrong I had everything.

Fresh Evidence.
Sunday December 4th
1512hrs

ON MY WAY TO gran's house, with my head filled with conflicting thoughts, my phone rang. It didn't connect to the in-car system though because it wasn't my car. Keeping one eye on the road, sort of, I fumbled in my bag with my left hand, fishing around until I found my phone and could glance at the screen.

PC Jan Van Dorn was calling me. I thumbed the button to answer the call, then looked back up and saw I was leaving my lane because the country road was going around a bend and I was not. I swore loudly and only just about had enough presence of mind to do so in Jane's voice.

'Um, hi?' said Jan. 'Everything okay that end?'

'Sorry,' I blushed. 'What can I do for you? Has there been a development?'

'With the Biddenden Lake case? Yes. Can you come to the station?'

'Right now?'

'Now would be good. Chief Inspector Quinn is here. I can't say much over the phone, but it would be in your best interest to drop whatever you are doing and get here if you can.'

'Um.' I was in a car with almost everything I owned. I could go anywhere and do anything. The route back from West Farleigh to gran's house in Aylesford took me through Maidstone so it would be easy to go straight there. 'I can probably be there in ten minutes. Can someone be informed I am coming or be waiting for me at the front desk? I got messed around a bit last time.'

'Really? Who messed you around?' he asked, his voice filled with surprise.

'The desk sergeant,' I admitted in a quiet voice, my bold confidence eroded by acknowledging I had no power in his environment.

Jan made a disgruntled noise and asked, 'Do you remember his name?'

If I had I wouldn't have told Jan; I didn't need him to fight my battles, nice though that might be. As it was, I couldn't dredge the name from my memory so I didn't have to lie about it. Jan said he would meet me at the front desk though, so we disconnected and I drove the rest of the distance wondering what the new development in the case might be and how this would change my involvement.

Maidstone Police Station. Sunday, December 4th 1530hrs

JAN MET ME AS promised but the unpleasant desk sergeant from Friday wasn't there anyway. The female police officer from Friday was though and I got a curt nod from her as Jan led me through the door and into the station. As he walked with me, he said, 'I like your hair. Did you get it done this morning?'

'Oh, um, yeah. Sort of.'

'Well, it suits you. Very, um... pink.'

'Thank you.' Jan smiled down at me with the curious grin he often wore and looking up at him with a smile of my own I walked into a wastepaper bin. I landed flat on my face like a clutz.

'Wow. Are you okay?' He asked, kneeling to offer me a hand up.

'Yeah,' I lied, rubbing my chin, 'just peachy.' Back on my feet, I asked about the Sandman case and if he had found any similar murders or reported incidents.

'Sorry,' he looked disappointed. 'The chief is riding all of us pretty hard. I can't talk about the case, but I haven't had time to divert any attention to the other issue. The chief is giving a briefing about it in about sixty seconds so I must hurry.' He apologized again and abandoned me at a desk to wait for his return.

Alone in a busy police station, I looked around self-consciously, though no-one paid me any attention.

Ten minutes ticked by and then another ten. I checked my phone yet again and drummed my fingers on the desk. I wanted to leave just to prove I didn't have to dance to the chief inspector's tune like everyone else around him, but I had no idea why I had been summoned so I stuck it out a little longer.

Just when my impatience was turning to anger, he appeared, coming through a door to my left with a gaggle of police officers around him. Jan was among them and managed to direct the chief inspector's attention my way. He changed direction to approach me. 'Ah, Miss Butterworth. Your firm's assistance will no longer be needed. Thank you.' And then he was moving again, forgetting me instantly.

I flapped my lips in surprise a couple of times but surprised myself when I stood up and shouted for him to stop.

His party all ground to a halt at once, several of his entourage sucking air between their teeth as if I had just kicked a sleeping dog. The chief inspector slowly wheeled around to face me. 'Could you repeat that please?' he said politely, placing the clipboard he carried behind his back so he presented a dignified and unthreatening pose.

I wasn't fooled though. This was his pond and he liked being the big fish in it. I was going to lose this exchange, but with Jan watching I intended to lose well. 'I asked who you thought you were, chief inspector.'

He chuckled in response, confident enough that he didn't bother to look at any of his subordinates for their mutual mirth. 'You ask me who I am and name me in the same sentence. Are you a buffoon? Please don't bother me any further. You will be paid for your time thus far. Good day, Miss Butterworth.'

'Who will you call next time, chief inspector?' he had been turning away again but stopped so he could look at me. 'This is far from the first time the Blue Moon Agency has provided the solution to a case that perplexed you. Shall I name the recent cases, or will you concede the point?' I didn't wait for an answer though. 'You asked for our assistance because you needed it, hiring our resource as specialists, but now you wish to dismiss me and do so rudely without providing any explanation as to why.'

Chief Inspector Quinn waited for me to finish, never showing any inclination to interrupt. It was a trait Tempest would most likely applaud because it was gentlemanly, but I knew he was using the time to craft his response. 'Miss Butterworth,' he started, hitting the *Miss* extra hard so I knew he was threatening to use my genderfluidity against me if he had to. 'The case has changed. It is a police investigation and I have no requirement to tell you anything. You were given an opportunity to investigate the case and a complete copy of the casefile. As I understand it, you have been able to add no value whatsoever.'

'It hasn't even been forty-eight hours yet,' I protested, but I sensed I was somehow now on the back foot.

'I thought you were specialists,' he scoffed. 'Were you not, in fact, pursuing an entirely different case last night?' He had me. If I admitted that I was he would claim I wasn't committed, if I denied it had any impact on my ability to pursue the Biddenden Lake case, he would call me a liar or an incompetent. Seeing he had won, he nodded his head at me. 'Good day, Miss Butterworth.'

Dammit. I gritted my teeth knowing anything I said now would just make things worse and slumped into the chair again when he disappeared through a door on the far side of the room. I watched Jan go with him, hoping he would spare me a sympathetic glance. He didn't though and I was left sitting by myself in an alien environment, stewing in my own thoughts and wondering just what had happened in the case that resulted in Quinn dismissing us.

Thirty seconds ticked by and no one spoke to me or paid me any attention. No one was looking after me or telling me whether I was expected to wait for Jan to return so I could be escorted out. So, I put my phone back into my handbag and stood up.

No one even looked my way.

I crossed the open plan office to the briefing room the chief inspector had been in.

No one paid me any attention.

Shrugging at their indifference, I pushed open the door to the briefing room and went inside. The room was empty but the briefing CI Quinn had just given was still on the screen. With a glance at the door in case a SWAT team were about to come in and clobber me, I clicked the mouse to bring it to life and took the presentation notes back to the start.

There had been a third murder.

I skim read the information as quickly as I could but it was very quickly clear that a third police officer from Kent had gone missing and had been subsequently found dead at Biddenden Lake. Another drowning, another set of weird bite marks and very few clues. The police had finally made the connection with the dating site though. I knew Meet Market from previous research and knew they had a specialist uniform section where girls or guys that wanted to date someone in uniform could focus their efforts on finding just that. I guess it made it popular though I imagined they were about to have some kind of court injunction thrown at them so the police could see who each of the three dead men had interacted with.

Well, stuff waiting for the courts to catch up. I was going to hack them tonight. Incensed by Quinn's dismissal and put down, I was more determined than ever to solve this case. My rising excitement died though when I remembered I had no clue why the cops were being targeted, how they were being killed and who might be behind it.

'Come on, Jane,' I said to myself. 'You have to be better than that.' I knew that neither Tempest nor Amanda had instant answers when they started a case. They always worked it out though. What was it Tempest always said? "Start by asking who benefits." I could hear his voice in my head.

'Are you supposed to be in here?' asked a man's voice.

I turned to see the unpleasant desk sergeant from Friday. 'Probably not,' I said with a sweet smile. I had all I needed, or at least, I appeared to know as much as the police did, so feeling like a real gumshoe, I ducked under his sneer as he held the door open for me and followed his insistent instructions to find the exit and leave.

Getting back into Tempest's Porsche and feeling the vibration of the meaty engine, I thought about my weekend. It was dark out and it was Sunday night so, like everyone else, I would be going to work in just a few hours when Monday morning rolled around. I hadn't had any time off yet though but had been dumped by my boyfriend, chased by a man with an erection, beaten up Karen's poor neighbour, and then had to flee from a house fire plus my car was now a burnt-out mess.

Despite all that, I had a smile on my face and felt like I had purpose. It had been my intention to head for home but I had other plans now, one of which was to check out the lake for myself. The casefile had maps in it. The spots the first two bodies were found were marked, and further marks suggested where they might have entered the water.

It would be dark soon, but I wasn't going to let that put me off.

Biddenden Lake. Sunday, December 4th 1648hrs

IT WAS JUST ABOUT full dark when I stopped in the car park next to a pay meter. Tempest's Porsche wasn't the only car in the car park, there were quite a few to my surprise, but perhaps it was more popular with anglers and such than Frank claimed.

The parking meter was busted, so with no way to pay, I set off with my phone in hand. I really wasn't sure what I might find here; damp grass and overgrown shrubs most likely, but maybe I would get a feel for the place also.

The police report on the original drowning ended with a verdict of accidental death because they refused to accept a swamp monster or anything else had taken Ian Dexter and drowned him and they couldn't prove Jennifer had done it either. The single set of footprints was a big part of that, and the forensic analysis had clever tests to determine that the shoes size and weight of the person wearing them were the same in every instance. So Jennifer hadn't killed him and no one else had either but no one believed the accidental drowning thing because his body was so brutally attacked.

A worrying thought surfaced; what if there was a beastie living here that had attacked Ian Dexter? I used to believe in all of this stuff. The whole mythical world was one I could get excited about. Growing up I had been such an ordinary kid and fantasised about being turned into a vampire or a werewolf because it would make me cool and interesting. Over time, Tempest convinced me that none of it was real at all and went on to prove it almost every day. Frank, on the other hand, was waiting for Tempest to be wrong.

A duck quacked loudly near my foot as I almost trod on it. It made me jump and catch my breath. 'What are you doing out here, Jane?' I asked aloud. Cold, spooky lakes were not the place to hang out if you have ever watched a horror film. Thinking that maybe I should just go, especially since I couldn't see anything in the dark despite the light on my phone, I turned around again.

Then I saw it. A flash of light near the water's edge. It came from a point maybe three or four-hundred yards away but as I squinted, it happened again. Unable to resist, I moved toward it.

I got within one-hundred yards and could begin to make out the sound of voices drifting over the still water. Another duck quacked but I ignored it as I pressed on.

Fifty yards and the silhouetted shapes of people were discernable whenever the light flared. I worried about getting too much closer, but I needed to find out what was going on. Who would be out here doing weird stuff in the dark unless they were up to no good? Could I call Jan for backup? Did I need to know more or would finding out more only reveal that I was in the company of killers and then get murdered myself?

I looked down at my phone and then felt my dread rising as I saw my mistake: I had the light on. It was shining for all to see and they must have spotted me coming from halfway around the lake.

Too late. A gruff voice came from behind me. 'Now what's a young lady like you doing out here by yourself?'

I spun around to see who was there and shone my light up to blind them, it was knocked from my hand by another unseen person and vanished in the long grass. Now blind myself since I had not developed any night vision, I stood my ground though my knees were shaking.

'What do you want?' I asked, trying my best to keep the quiver from my voice.

'I should ask you the same thing,' said the man that had first spoken. 'You were in Frank's shop today. Did you follow me here?' He stepped in closer to me, his face now visible in the moonlight. I recognized him as the man that Frank gave the box to: the man from the Kent League of Demonologists.

'Yes,' the man said, almost purring. 'Yes, you are interested in the arcane arts, are you not?' He turned his head to the side to speak with someone I couldn't see in the dark. 'Lionel, we have a new pledge.'

'What, I, um, no,' I stuttered.

'Come witness our ritual, child. We shall summon this water demon and dispatch it.'

'Hold on a moment,' said a new voice that was probably Lionel, 'She can't be a new pledge, Jerome, she's a girl. The league has been a bastion of male demonologists for centuries.'

'They have a woman in Caithness. She was sworn in as a full member almost four years ago,' argued Jerome.

'Scotland? Who gives a stuff about what they get up to in Scotland?' Lionel wasn't letting this go.

I tried to speak up. 'I haven't followed you from the shop. I'm not interested in joining your club.'

Just as Lionel got into his face, Jerome said, 'Men are talking, dear. We'll get to you in a moment. If you want to join the league, you'll have to know your place.'

'She's not joining,' insisted Lionel. At that point I decided they were a couple of idiots, spotted my phone and left them to it.

Another flash of light drew my attention to the lake once more. The rest of the league, for that is who I assumed they were, were gathered at the water's edge. My phone was tucked away and the light turned off anyway as I neared them. I didn't think they could see me coming but I was doing my best to move stealthily. A bush provided a handy place from which to watch.

Near the water, half a dozen shadows were doing something complicated. Every few seconds a spark danced across the water and died. I still couldn't see much but there was another bush a few yards closer to them. I scrambled to it, keeping low, then popped my head up again.

Above me the clouds moved and moonlight poured through again, reflecting off the lake to show me the men. One was holding a large book. It was open and looked heavy and reminded me of a large bible, the ornate type you might find being used in a church for services. Another man was holding a crucifix and as I watched, I saw, to my horror, that two of them had swords.

Then a hand grabbed my shoulder painfully. 'Spying ain't lady like, you know.' It was Lionel, who must have bested Jerome because there was no sign of him.

'Let go,' I protested, flailing at his arm, but he held my coat in a vicelike grip and was far stronger than me.

He dragged me into the open as he shouted to his colleagues, 'Hey, gents. We have a spy. She followed that careless nitwit Jerome here from the shop in Rochester.'

'Bring her forward,' boomed a deep voice from the lake's edge.

I kicked out at Lionel, connecting with a knee and he stumbled. He didn't go down though and quickly corrected himself before delivering a hard jab to my ribs. 'If you won't behave like a lady, I won't feel any need to treat you like one,' he snarled at me.

The blow knocked the breath out of me and weakened my ability to fight him off. It was moot though because we were already at the lake's edge and mere yards from the rest of the league.

With a rough shove, Lionel let go of my coat finally but thrust me toward the center of the small group who had already fanned out.

A spokesman, the one with the deep voice, addressed me. 'Why do you spy on us, child?'

I glanced about at the men. They were all facing me but more than half of them had their faces shrouded in darkness as they faced away from the moon. I couldn't decide if they intended me any harm or not, but if Lionel was anything to go by, they might just give me a beating for the heck of it.

'I was curious about what I was seeing. That's all.'

'So you're here by accident are you?' scoffed Lionel. 'Pull the other one, love.'

'Not by accident, no. I was hired by the police to assist their investigation into the recent drownings.'

The man with the deep voice questioned that. 'They hired you? Why? Who are you?'

This was going to be tricky to answer depending on their opinion of Tempest. 'I work at Blue Moon.'

There was a moment of worrying quiet, then a raucous burst of laughter from deep voice. 'Well, I'll be blowed!' he roared. The rest of the men joined in, all except Lionel, who, still standing a bit too close to me, merely harrumphed. 'She's one of the non-believers,' deep voice cackled, still finding the revelation of my employment funny.

A man to his left turned to deep voice to address him, 'Grand Mage, what shall we do with her?'

As the laughter died down, the Grand Mage wiped tears from his eyes. 'We show her. That's what we do. That fool Tempest Michaels and his daft investigation agency are overdue a surprise. So, let's show this young lady the beast in the lake and see her deny its existence when it tries to bite her face off.'

Before I could work out what he meant by that, I was grabbed on either side and wrestled toward the water. 'You'll make great bait, missy,' laughed Lionel, his awful breath in my face as he manhandled me toward the edge of the lake.

'Don't worry, miss,' the Grand Mage assured me in his deep voice, you'll only be bait to lure it in. We won't actually let it bite you.'

Lionel leaned in close to whisper, 'I might let it have a nibble though. Just to teach you a lesson.'

With two men holding me in place, my feet were right at the edge of the water and struggling against them did nothing but expend more energy. Next to me, they were setting up their odd ritual again, the intermittent sparks dancing over the water while the man with the book began chanting.

I figured this would go on for a while, but hoped they would get bored when nothing happened, release me and go home.

A minute went by. Then two. Then something disturbed the surface of the water twenty yards off the shore. It was directly in front of me and my pulse beat a staccato rhythm as I decided not only was it not a fish, it was coming in a straight line, directly for me.

Then I saw another movement to the left of the first and started to panic, wriggling against the strong hands holding me.

'Be ready,' hissed the Grand Mage prompting the sound of swords being drawn from scabbards.

Then, from the water, in an explosion of weed and muck and spray, a man in scuba gear emerged, and right next to him, another one. They both held powerful looking crossbows, the black frames gleaming in the moonlight like obsidian.

'What the devil?' asked the Grand Mage. His next question, if he had one, was cut off by a whistle blast and the grip on my arms loosened as Lionel and whoever else was holding began looking about to see what was going on.

Banshee cries filled the night as figures emerged from the blackness, all kitted out in survivalist kit. Some looked to be wearing night vision goggles. It was enough to convince Lionel I was no longer a priority and I yanked my arms free as the two men turned their attention to the new threat.

I had no idea what was going on and no particular interest in finding out. I was going home. Stuff the rest of them. Taking a meaningful step forward, I slipped on a rock, tried to correct myself, over corrected, slipped again and landed on my arse in the water.

I wasn't in deep, but I had a wet bum and wet knickers and my boots were filling with water. A scant few yards ahead of me, the crazy Kent League of Demonologists were now surrounded by what looked like a special forces team, except they didn't have guns because this is England.

A standoff was taking place, and no one was saying anything. The Grand Mage had a haughty look and his arms crossed as if he was expecting an apology and explanation for the disturbance.

The battle of silence ended when the leader of the special forces team pulled off his balaclava and spoke, 'Stand down, men.' As all around him the crossbows were lowered, and the swords, which had been raised in defensive poses, also began to droop, he sighed. 'I really thought we had something this time.'

'Who the devil are you, young man,' demanded the Grand Mage sounding impatient and annoyed.

The special forces leader stepped forward. 'Lieutenant Colonel Antswith-George at your service, sir. I apologise for the surprise. My men are trained to battle the forces of hell. We are God's ultimate fighting force.'

'Well, you just ruined an ancient ritual that would have lured the beast in this lake to its demise at the hands of my men, a secret league of demonologists sworn to protect the realm of men against all evil.'

The lieutenant colonel's nose twitched. 'It's not a very secret league though, is it?'

'How so?' the Grand Mage snapped.

'Well, you just told me and all my men about it for one. Hard to keep a secret when you announce it the moment you meet someone, wouldn't you say.'

The Grand Mage was working up to full bluster when I interrupted. 'I heard about you today in Rochester High Street. It's not a secret at all.' I didn't need to add my two-penneth but they deserved it. Plus, I was upset about my wet bum and wasn't sure I would find anything in the car to put under it to protect Tempest's seat.

The Grand Mage was reaching apoplectic rage levels, no doubt his head turning red if one had sufficient light to see it by. 'Well, I never.'

If he had more to say, I didn't hear it. Bored with the entire escapade, I was cold and wet and wanted to go to gran's house now. I wasn't sure if the special forces team would try to stop me but I announced loudly, 'I'm not with them, I was just their bait,' as I walked away and they let me pass through their midst without comment.

I had to orientate myself to find my way back to the car park, which was further away than I thought, and I squelched in my sodden boots every step of the way. At the car, I rooted around to find something I could sit on so I wouldn't ruin his beautiful suede seats. Settling on a collection of plastic bags, I got the engine on and the heaters working and pointed the nose toward home.

Visiting the lake had not been a great idea.

Late Night Research. Sunday, December 4th 2246hrs

THE THING ABOUT RESEARCH is you never know what it is you are going to find. Tempest always makes a point of complimenting me on my ability to find information he would have thought unobtainable, or of piecing together sufficient information to provide the answer hidden among the mess. I had never really understood what he meant until I was doing it in a bid to answer my own questions.

Gran had let me in but hadn't helped to bring my belongings into the house. I hadn't asked her to either. She was a tenacious old bird when she wanted to be, but at eighty-four she was not about to try out for the England Cricket Team. As I ferried items from the car, she relaxed in front of the television with a cup of tea. The England rugby team were beating five bells out of Scotland and she didn't want to be disturbed until it was over. The trip back and forth to the car was more than one hundred yards each way because Aylesford was so old the one-way street was designed for horses and the space between did not allow for parked cars. It took a while to get it all in, but as promised, gran had a bed waiting for me. It was upstairs in her tiny cottage, but it was all mine, it was rent free and there was little danger I would get kicked out at any point.

Leaving her to watch the rugby, I shoved clothes in the tiny wardrobe, hung them on the handles of the window and stuffed them anywhere I could find that wasn't on the bed or the small table I intended to use as a computer desk.

It was a bit cramped but half an hour after getting it all in, my screens sprang into life and I was in business. Okay, two of the screens were balanced on books stacked up to the right height, and my mouse barely had room to move, but it was working.

I cracked my knuckles in preparedness to start, then changed my mind and went downstairs to check on gran and get a cup of tea. Halftime had just finished so she was back in her armchair, which she appeared to have bought in the fifties, and had a ready meal dinner on a plate with what looked suspiciously like a gin and tonic next to it.

I eyed the ready meal. Gran thought cooking for one was too much hassle so she rarely bothered. I would be dusting off my meagre culinary skills though to do my best at keeping her well-fed. I could provide the groceries too since she insisted I would pay no rent.

I had intended to ask if she wanted a cup of tea but I thought her answer obvious so just made one for myself and went back upstairs.

When gran called out to say she was going to the pub to see Mavis, I looked at the clock to see more than an hour had slipped by. The pub was next door but one, so gran only had about twelve yards to wobble each way. I offered to escort her nevertheless, but she scoffed at the notion, saying she had been making her own way there since she moved in sixty-five years ago.

My cup of tea sat cold and untouched, my focus too absorbed by what I was doing. By the time gran returned at nine o'clock I had access to Meet Market. Finding and accessing their details had been tougher than I thought, the Meet Market firewall requiring patience and tenacity to get through undetected.

Once in, my hope soared as I dared to believe I might instantly find a single woman who had contacted all three, arranged dates with all three and who would be the instant prime suspect for their murders. It wasn't to be though.

Gran interrupted me just before nine-thirty when she said she was going to bed. I kissed her on the cheek and thanked her once more for putting a roof over my head. My concentration broken, I decided to change out of my clothes and into something more comfortable. I was tired and thirsty but I was also making headway so I wasn't stopping.

With my tea refreshed and pyjamas on, I settled in front of the screens once more. Each of the men had been in contact with several women, playing the odds perhaps but a lot of the conversations between each man and several different women all overlapped making it very difficult to work out who they might have met with on their fateful nights.

Getting frustrated by it, I pushed the open tabs to one side and started a new search. I needed to track down Karen Gilbert and thankfully that task proved far easier. Using her social media profile I was able to find her sister and several friends, clone the account of one woman that appeared as a friend on everyone else's profile and then send messages from within the system that would look like it was coming from someone in the group. The only way I could get caught out was if the friend whose account I had cloned was actually with people when I sent a fake message from her.

I got lucky on my third message though, when Megan told Wendy that Karen was staying with Matilda because Karen had left her stove on and burned her house down. That Karen hadn't told her friend she had a crazed stalker who might follow her didn't surprise me. Now all I had to do was find a full name for Matilda, use that to find an address from the post office and then use that to get a phone number from directory enquiries.

It took me almost forty seconds.

It was getting late when I made the phone call, but I had to be sure that Karen was safe. Having gone to stay with a friend, I suspected she wouldn't be taking any precautions which might expose her if the Sandman was keeping close tabs on her or tracking her somehow.

'Hello,' said a voice I didn't know. I wasn't expecting Karen because I called the house number for the friend but I got a man anyway.

I set my voice to normal and delivered the lie, 'Good evening, this is Detective Sergeant Inkwell of Kent Police. To whom am I speaking please?'

'Err,' caught by surprise, like I knew he would be, the man was instantly wondering what the right answer was. 'It's ah, Geoff Carpenter.'

Jolly good. I tracked down Matilda Carpenter so I had the right place. 'I need to speak with Karen Gilbert. Is she there, please?'

'She, ah, she went to bed already,' Mr Carpenter stammered. 'Is it urgent?'

'Yes, sir. I'm afraid it is. I must insist you wake her up.' I could hear the man muttering something but not make out what it was. However, the sound of footsteps on stairs told me he was doing as I asked.

Another voice appeared in the background. 'Where do you think you're going Geoffrey?' It had to be the man's wife because she was talking to him like he was a child.

'I have the police on the line. They want to talk to Karen?' he explained.

'So you thought you would just let yourself into her room did you? Hoping to catch her half-dressed?' The woman's tone was impatient, as if she was always catching the man doing things she didn't approve of and this was just one more example.

'No, love,' he began to protest, but she cut him off again.

'Give me the phone,' she demanded, and I was not one little bit surprised when her voice boomed in my ear. 'Who is this?'

I found myself feeling sorry for Geoffrey, but calmly answered. 'This is Detective Sergeant...' oh, no! I had forgotten the name of the police officer I invented. I tried to fill in the blank but I had left it too long.

'Can't remember your own name then. Is this one of Geoffrey's silly friends from the pub. Did he put you up to this so he could get a look at my friend in bed? Was he going to take pictures?' I could hear her draw a breath to really start laying into me when yet another voice appeared in the background.

'What is all this racket?' asked Karen Gilbert.

114

In the heartbeat between Matilda drawing breath and the next tirade of abuse I quickly shouted, 'It's Jane,' in my normal voice in the hope that Karen would hear me.

It felt like I was taking part in a pantomime but everyone had a script except me. There was muffled mumbling but a few seconds later, Karen finally answered the phone. 'Are you a girl or a boy this time?'

'Please, just don't hang up,' I begged. 'I found out some information on the Sandman.'

There was a pause before she said, 'Alright, I'm listening.'

I told her about the other Sandman case I found earlier. I didn't want to freak her out, but I felt it best to scare her into being on high alert; it might save her life. It had been my hope to draw CI Quinn's attention to the case but that went down in flames before it even got into the air. Tempest and Amanda would be back tomorrow though and it gave me hope that together our combined effort might be able to solve the case for her, catch the maniac and make her safe again.

Karen was shocked by my news but also relieved that she had come forward to seek help when she did. Before she hung up, she apologized for judging me and for avoiding me; how I dressed was not her concern nor should it blight her opinion she said.

With the call finished and an important task complete, I stifled yet another yawn and went back to looking at the Biddenden Lake case. There were so many aspects to explore though. The dead police officers were linked by their involvement on the original swamp monster case but that could be nothing but coincidence. They were also all on Meet Market, which seemed more significant. Tempest's first question of who stands to gain wasn't yielding any answers; I could not come up with any benefit from the deaths.

So I went back to the start and looked at the original case. The investigation three years ago was led by Chief Inspector Quinn, but I already knew that. He had a team of three officers working for him, all of whom were now dead. There were other officers involved in lesser roles but when I looked at the central team, the connection no longer looked coincidental.

That took me back to asking who would benefit from their deaths? The only motive I came up with was revenge on the part of Jennifer, but I got no sense of that from her when we spoke. Sure, she was angry at the police for the way she was accused and treated. Ultimately though, she was released and was getting on with her life.

The case file contained photographs taken at the lake, some of which were of the body and quite grim in their nature. Ian Dexter had died brutally with large chunks of flesh torn from his back and arms and legs. The cause of death was recorded as drowning but I was sure he would have died from blood loss equally. More photographs showed footprints where little numbered flags identified them, and a measure recorded length and width. There were casts made of the footprints at the scene and photographs of the casts in the case file. I knew Jennifer's lawyer had been able to dismiss the concept of an accomplice, the only way she could have killed Ian Dexter, because only two sets of footprints were found at the scene. The footprints were a key piece of evidence which Quinn had used to enforce the idea only Jennifer could be the killer. It backfired on him though, her lawyer turning the concept around because she couldn't swim and there was no way she could overpower him. If there was no accomplice, then she had to be innocent and the ground at the lake was too soft for anyone else to have approached without leaving their own set of prints.

Was there a piscine beast in Biddenden Lake? The press hadn't got hold of the story yet, the police doing an effective job of keeping it under wraps. For how long though? Someone leaked the drawing the first time around, and that was a point; someone in the police, someone linked to the case, had leaked a drawing to the press. In exchange for money seemed the likely reason, but who was the person guilty of that?

I went around in circles for another half an hour but in the end had to admit that I wasn't getting anywhere. The case constructed by Chief Inspector Quinn was convincing but contained no actual evidence. Jennifer's DNA was on Ian Dexter but they were in a relationship so that meant nothing. She had no signs of injury which, given the state of the victim, there would have been had she been responsible.

Putting it to one side, I focused on the Meet Market site. The number of women who had been in contact with the three men in the period leading up to their deaths totaled fifty-seven. I wanted to ignore those that had sent just one or just a couple of messages but then considered that maybe not getting the response they wanted was enough to make them kill. Stranger things had happened. So, I started to create a profile for each woman. I didn't really have a goal in mind, it just felt like a thing to do if I was being thorough. There was almost no cross over though. My hope was that I would find a single woman with the face of a pyscho bunny-boiler who had contacted all three victims and arranged to meet them at times and dates that coincided with their disappearances.

No such luck though. I managed to find two women who had messaged more than one of the three men, but one was rather plain looking and hadn't even garnered responses from either man, and the other was a pretty blonde but wanted to talk about quilting and cross-stitch so was soon ignored. I kept going but it felt like the Meet Market thing was a dead end.

Two more hours had passed, and my back was beginning to hurt from the lack of movement. There was a lot to do yet, but I had to sleep. I twisted and stretched in place, trying to unkink my neck and shoulders, then, as I ran the shut down program and turned off the three monitors one by one, someone sitting behind me sneezed and I screamed like I was being murdered.

Cardiac Trauma. Monday, December 5th 0154hrs

LYING ON THE FLOOR, hoping my heart would recover from the shock, I looked up at the bed. The sneeze came from a large black cat which was now staring lazily over the edge of the bed at me and licking its nose.

A quiet knock on the door preceded the handle turning and gran's wrinkled face appearing around the edge of the door as it opened. 'Are you alright, love?'

'Cat,' I managed.

Gran squinted where my hand was pointed. 'Ah, yes. That's just Fuddyduddy from next door. He's always sneaking in here because they have kids now. Come on Fuddyduddy,' she cooed as she scooped him under one arm. 'You should get some sleep, love. You've got work in the morning.'

When the door shut, I could still hear gran chatting away to the cat who was probably going to be quite happy tucked up on gran's bed.

'Will there be anymore surprises?' I asked the room. I decided not to tempt fate and look for skeletons in my closet, opting instead to get under the covers and fall into a dreamless and very deep sleep until my alarm went off at six-thirty.

Full Office. Monday, December 5th 0834hrs

USUALLY I AM THE first to work. This is partly because unlike the other two, I don't go to the gym most mornings, but it is also by design as I like to be the first in. When I slid Tempest's Porsche into the carpark at 0834hrs, the first thing I could see was the tail end of Amanda's mini sticking out, so she was here already and the lights in both the rear offices were on.

And the windows were open. Why were the windows open? Neither Tempest nor Amanda were visible in their offices, so with a disappointed final pat, I said goodbye to Tempest's car and opened the back door to go in.

Then the smell hit me, and I gagged. I had forgotten the fish! The two rotten fish I left in ziplock bags in the storeroom. In such a rush last night, I left them there hoping the plastic would contain the smell so I could deal with them later. Actually, my plan had been to ask Tempest about them because I didn't want to turn all the evidence over to the police, but my fog-filled brain forgot them completely.

From inside I could hear exaggerated shouts and excitement. They were going to kill me! Since running away wasn't much of an option, I took a deep breath and ran inside. The corridor that links the back door with the rest of the office also led to the storeroom. Both the door for it and the door for the main office were propped open.

119

'We're going to have to open the back door to create a through draft,' Tempest yelled at Amanda as he came back through the front door. I didn't know where he had just been but he had an unhappy look on his face and was holding his hands out like he wanted them to be somewhere else. Had he just got rid of the fish? He spotted me hovering near the back of the office and gave me a wave. 'We found some fish.'

The Dachshunds spotted me as well, so I was trying to look sorry and guilty while also petting the two dogs as they fussed around my feet with their tails buzzing.

Amanda said, 'Good morning, Jane.'

'Hey, guys. How was France?' I tried weakly.

'We'll catch up in a minute,' Tempest said. 'First we need to air the office out and get rid of this smell. You can tell us about the fish over a coffee shortly.'

I wasn't getting the cold shoulder treatment thankfully. They were just being efficient. The next twenty minutes passed quickly as Amanda sent me out to buy desiccant to absorb the smell and air freshener to mask it for now. I told them where the fish had come from and its method of arrival. They looked a little surprised, but it wasn't the first time the firm had received intimidating messages. Unfortunately, the fish were gone; Tempest chased a rubbish truck down the road and threw the ziplock bags into it just before it drove away.

It was cold in the office from the breeze flowing through, but the doors and windows were shut again making me hopeful that warmth would return soon. I wasn't going to moan about it, that was for sure. Tempest looked up from the coffee machine now that it was finally time for the office to settle into a routine. So far as he was concerned, the fish thing was in the past. He even apologized for losing my evidence.

To move things on, I asked a work question, 'You haven't asked me to raise an invoice for the Yeti case yet, boss. Will there be one?'

Tempest grinned a big grin. 'Not this time. We got paid in cash and got a bonus. And that was on top of getting our trip for free. I need to deposit the money today though; it feels like too much to be carrying around.'

'I still need to account for it though, right?' I was asking the questions carefully. If Tempest wanted to start doing cash stuff off the book and robbing the tax man that was his business. It would be a new version of Tempest though if he did.

Thankfully, he laughed at the idea. 'Goodness, no. It all needs to be accounted for properly.'

The coffee machine bleeped and filled the first cup which he handed to me. 'Amanda,' he called through to her office. 'You would like a coffee?'

'Damned skippy,' came her reply.

As Tempest arranged a second porcelain cup, his attention on the machine, he said, 'We need to catch up on recent events. No doubt you have a log of cases that came in while we were away, and I believe you have been looking into some of them yourself?'

He said it as a question, the cadence darting upwards as the sentence ended. 'Yes to everything,' I replied. You'll find a log of cases in a file marked caselog when you open your desktop. Amanda has the same file so you'll want to discuss who is going to tackle what.'

'I'm taking the werewolf thing in Whitstable,' Amanda shouted through before either Tempest or I could say another word.

We looked at each other. Tempest had Amanda's coffee in his hand. I sipped mine and kept quiet. 'Why is that?' Tempest asked as he walked across the office to deliver her drink.

'I saw it first.' I heard her reply though I couldn't see her. 'You snooze you lose,' she added. 'Because I like Whitstable. Take your pick. Or it could be mine because...' I didn't hear the rest of what she said because she dropped her voice to a whisper, but I got the general gist from the flushed look Tempest had when he came back out of her office. At some point we were going to have to deal with the obvious fact that they were in a relationship now. I just hoped it didn't blow up in their faces as it would make the work environment rather awkward.

Trying to pick up where we left off, I continued with, 'Just in case you have forgotten, you have an invitation to Lord Hale's party next weekend. You replied but have not confirmed the names of those that will be attending. He requested that you bring up to twelve guests including yourself.'

A burst of steam to clear the nozzle announced that Tempest was done making coffee. He turned around and stood up again, this time his focus on the tiny white cup which he had under his nose. He whispered something to it which sounded disturbingly like, 'My precious,' then tipped it back and downed the cup in one go.

'That was actually a bit too hot,' he said. I drank mine and handed him the cup. 'Now what were you saying about Lord Hale?'

'The party next weekend. Lord Hale, well probably not actually Lord Hale but his butler or something, has been pestering me to give him the names of the guests who will be attending. Up to twelve guests and I think they were leaning toward there being more rather than less attending.'

He nodded as he considered the information. 'Yes, this is quite the pay day too. All to do with some monster or creature or something that has visited his family and killed the incumbent lord on his eightieth birthday. His birthday is this weekend and he wants us there to ensure he lives through it.' Tempest was recalling the information from memory but he had it about right. 'I want to attend, not least because he is offering so much money for an easy weekend of dinner and relaxing.' He turned his head toward the back of the office. 'Amanda.'

'What?'

'Do you have plans for next weekend?'

'Why?'

He flipped his eyebrows, gave up shouting and went to her office. I followed. It was interesting how their dynamic had changed in the days they had been absent. Where they were both a little coy with each other, treading carefully and being observant of the other person's sensibilities, now they were more like a couple that had been married for a decade.

Leaning against her doorframe with his hands hooked over the architrave above, he said, 'I am going to that party at Lord Hale's mansion next weekend. I thought you might wish to join me. For the money he is paying, it ought to be more than just me attending. I think Big Ben will come if I ask him. It's free food and drink and I can tell him there will be girls there.'

'Will there be?' she asked.

'Shouldn't think so.'

She stared at him from her chair and I watched as a cheeky smile played across her face. 'I could invite Patience, you know.'

Tempest sucked in a breath of surprise. 'Oh, that's naughty. Let's do it. We can have them arranged as a couple.'

Amanda's eyes were sparkling with mischief. 'Big Ben will not be pleased.'

'No,' cackled Tempest. 'He'll go nuts, but Patience will be my friend for life.'

'What's going on?' I asked, confused by their exchange. I knew the people they were talking about but quite why setting one up with the other was funny I had no idea.

Tempest glanced at Amanda, then turned to me so he could explain. 'Big Ben and Patience have a little history. She likes him but he prides himself on never, um...'

'He never sleeps with the same woman twice,' Amanda finished the sentence for him. 'Patience is apparently the only one to have achieved that feat in years and she is hungry for more.'

'So you are going to set them up because it will be funny?' I confirmed.

'Yup,' they said simultaneously.

Tempest took out his phone and opened a note. 'Who else do we invite? It's a big night at a manor house. It could be fun.'

Amanda turned back to her computer. 'I don't know many couples. Just single girls and I'm not letting them anywhere near Big Ben. You could invite Frank though, it sounds weird so he'll love it. I don't know if he has a plus one but knowing him, he'll turn up with a Wookie or the invisible man or something. It might be fun to have a group though; I get on well with Jagjit and Alice,' Amanda said, referring to one of Tempest's oldest friends and his new wife. It was their honeymoon they had crashed in France when the Yeti showed up.

'Sure. I'll have a think about it and see who wants to come.' Tempest slid his phone back into a pocket and backed away from Amanda's office. 'Before I get on with anything else, let's have a catch up on the last week, yes?'

The question was directed at me so the two of us settled into the couches in the reception/waiting area and I went through what had been happening, taking him all the way back to Annabelle Forsythe and her brush with the vampire. Tempest nodded and paid attention, stopping me at one point so he could invite Amanda to come and listen too.

I was nervous about telling them what I had been doing because it was way outside of my job description and had I messed things up it might have embarrassed the firm. They didn't see it like that though; they thought I had grabbed the fumbled ball and run to the goal, or something like that. I'm not very good at sports analogies. They were seriously impressed that I had just grabbed a case and solved it and then didn't even feel the need to tell anyone about it. I kept it secret because I wasn't sure how they would react, but they thought I was just the coolest, most ego-in-control person they had ever met.

I sure felt good about sharing. So then I told them about the Sandman and getting almost burnt to death in Karen's little house. I finished that tale with a smile, and that was when I saw their expressions.

'The client's house got burnt down?' asked Amanda.

'Um,'

My attention swung to Tempest when he spoke. 'You're kidding right?'

'Um,'

Amanda said, 'Okay,' as she grimaced at Tempest and my head swung to look at her again. I felt like I was watching tennis. 'We need to get a grip on this now.'

'What's happening?' I asked, my worry starting to rise.

Tempest and Amanda stood up at the same time. 'I'll call the insurers,' Tempest said as he pulled out his phone.

Amanda's phone appeared in her hand as well. 'I need the name and number for the client.' Then she saw the panicked look on my face and let her shoulders relax. 'Look, it's probably nothing, but with a member of the firm on the premises, it would be easy for the client to argue that our presence was connected to the arson and we need to get ahead of that before it happens.'

I had my palms either side of my face. I was mortified. 'Oh, lord. I had no idea.'

'Don't sweat it,' Tempest said as he finished his call. 'The insurers are going to send over some forms for the client to sign. Essentially, she will sign away her right to sue us at a later date. Before I proceed though, I have to ask; is there any way that your presence at her house could have been a contributing factor in the arson attack?'

I shook my head instinctively, then said, 'Wait. I don't know. Maybe.' When they both looked at me, I shrugged. 'How can I tell?'

Tempest nodded and skewed his lips to one side and then the other as he thought. 'I'm going to discuss it with her and see where that leaves us. Do you have my car keys?'

'Ah, yeah, sure.' I fetched them from my bag, unhooking the shiny Porsche key from the others with a tinge of sadness.

Ten minutes later I was alone in the office and wanted something to kick. Tempest had called Karen Gilbert, charmed the pants off her and arranged to go directly to Matilda's house so he could see her. Amanda let him get on with it; he seemed to have it under control, but two minutes after he left, she went out as well. She had a case that was worth looking into and had already arranged to visit the prospective client.

Silently stewing over how my move from office admin assistant to paranormal detective had plummeted from triumph to miserable failure, I realised I hadn't even told them about the Biddenden Lake case. I wasn't going to call Tempest right now though, that was for sure.

My sullen mood was interrupted when the door opened. It was not long after nine o'clock so we were open for business and people did drop in from time to time. I fixed on my professional face to look up at the door. Coming through it though was some kind of giant beast.

Reformed Ogre. Monday, December 5th 0911hrs

TENSING IN MY CHAIR as adrenalin hit my system and told me I needed to run to the back door, the creature's face came around the edge of the door and said, 'Hello.' It was Arthur. I don't think he noticed the sigh of relief I exhaled, but his face crinkled with confusion as I fanned myself with a handy notebook. I was getting jumpy.

'Hello, Arthur. Good morning. You are looking well. I must say I like your new clothes.'

'Good morning,' he replied, then looked down at himself. Arthur was wearing a hat. Not a bobble hat or something he might have found in a second-hand shop, but a fedora. At least, I think the correct name for the style is a fedora. Whatever the case, he had on a new hat and it went with the full-length rain mac he wore and then I saw that he had on proper shoes. His beard was still a little unruly but it was washed and I couldn't see any bits of twig in it anymore. Where was the tramp I knew? He even had on a tie. As he doffed his hat, he said, 'You mean these old things? My tailor was always good at making things fit, I suppose.' I laughed at his joke; tramps with tailors. He was through the door now and checking it shut behind him as it was cold outside. 'Is this a good time?' He paused just inside the doorway and sniffed.

I stood up to speak with him rather than sit behind the desk. 'There was an incident with a fish,' I explained. 'A good time for what? What can I help you with?'

'I'm here to thank you, actually. You and Tempest. I don't know what I would have done without your help. Is he here?'

I looked at the giant bear of a man before me and felt both joy and sorrow. His was a sad tale but one which I hoped might now have a happier ending. 'He's not, I'm afraid,' I said to answer his question. 'He will be pleased to hear you are doing better though.'

'Yes. Yes, I am doing better, and I have you two to thank for that.' Then, with a lurching movement he reached forward to grab my right hand and got down on one knee.

Oh, my friggin' lord, he was about to propose. 'Arthur what are you doing?' I squeaked.

Looking directly at me, for down on one knee his head was now at the same height as mine, he said, 'I pledge to come to your aid should you ever need it. While I may always be an ogre, I am also Sir Arthur and I will defend and protect you against all evil. Should you ever need my help, I will answer your call. No quest will prove too demanding, no villain too terrible.'

Then the door opened again, and Jan walked in. He opened his mouth to speak then took in the scene before him and skidded to a stop. Arthur still had his hand in mine and was still in classic marriage proposal pose. Jan held up his hands and started to back out the door, apologizing with his eyes for interrupting.

I said, 'Stop.' The instruction aimed at Jan who was at the door and about to open it. He looked utterly bewildered. 'Arthur get up you great lummox. You are incredibly sweet, but I cannot imagine a scenario where I will need a reformed ogre to come to my rescue.' Arthur let go of my hand and pushed on his bent knee to get himself back upright. I saw Jan mouth the word, 'Wow!' as Arthur got to his full height.

The giant man smiled at me. 'When ever your call comes, I will be ready, Miss Jane. Do not forget; Sir Arthur is in your debt.' Then he bowed deeply, bid me a good day and left, Jan holding the door open to let him out.

'How big is that guy?' commented Jan once Arthur was gone. 'I've never seen a guy that big. Where the heck does he buy trousers?' Jan was in uniform today and he looked delicious. As Arthur left, Jan was peering over the frosted section of the glass front window to watch him walk down the street which meant I was presented with a perfect shot of his pert bottom.

When he turned around, I was still staring at the same spot, fantasizing a little, only now I was staring at his groin and he saw me do it. A grin broke out on his face.

I caught myself and blushed deeply, turning away to cover my embarrassment. My cheeks were getting overworked recently. 'Goodness, is it hot in here?' I asked as I fanned my face again to dissipate the heat radiating off it. Remembering that I didn't know why Jan was here, I asked him.

'Oh, I just wanted to clear the air after yesterday.'

'There's really no need,' I assured him, secretly glad he had come to see me even if he was doing it because he thought I was a girl.

'Well, I hadn't expected ol' Quinn to be so abrupt with you. I had no idea he was going to take you off the case. Of course, he doesn't have to share his plans with us lowly constables and I can assure you he doesn't.'

'Yes, well, it's done now.' I was thinking about how I was going to tell him I wasn't a girl, but I wasn't comfortable doing it. I suppose it sounds easy to do; 'Hey I'm actually a guy inside this cute dress.' Easy, right? It wasn't though. I hadn't ever had this problem before. The Jane personality was only a few months old and her development had taken time. The fake bra was only weeks old and the voice just as new. Until recently, it was easier to tell I was a guy, but I liked the full transformation and I wasn't going backwards now. I gave up and asked him a question instead. 'Listen, I have a question.'

He flipped his eyebrows to show he was listening. 'Go on.'

129

'Is anyone looking into whether this could be an inside job?' His confused face told me he didn't follow. 'I got a message to back off from the case yesterday. A threatening message,' I added just in case it hadn't been clear.

Now he frowned at me, coming forward to see if I was serious. 'Someone threatened you?'

I leaned back against my desk, putting one bum cheek on it. 'You notice the wonderful fishy aroma?' I asked.

Jan frowned again. 'Yeah? Oh, you mean that wasn't him?' he pointed over his shoulder. I had to concede that if I saw Arthur and detected a bad smell at the same time, I might connect the two things erroneously as well.

I shook my head. 'No, someone threw a pair of rotten fish at the office front window and they had a message inside them.'

'Inside the fish?'

'Inside the wrapping that went around the fish. They were... nevermind. The point is someone told me to back off.'

'What did the message say. Exactly, I mean. What were the exact words? Better yet, can I see it?'

'Yeah,' I drawled. 'There was a bit of an issue and the fish and the message is gone.'

'Gone?'

'Gone. Look, there's nothing I can do about the fish or the message. It said I should back off or I would suffer and the only case I have been looking into was the Biddenden Lake case. So, the question I started with was whether anyone was looking into the possibility that someone from the police is the killer. The victims are all police, the killings, assuming the first one is not connected, are copycat killings using the kind of detail no one from the public would know and I am being told to back off when the only people outside of the police who knew I was involved are my grandmother and Jennifer Lasseter.'

I could see he wasn't convinced. 'I get what you are saying,' he conceded. 'The answer though is no. Chief Inspector Quinn has not raised the idea that it could be one of our own and to my knowledge neither has anyone else.'

Was I barking up the wrong tree? 'What do you think?' I asked.

'About the killer being a cop? I need some time to think about it, but I suppose there is no reason to rule it out. My gut reaction says it won't be, I am struggling to work out what their motivation might be. That was true before though.'

'What about Jennifer Lasseter?'

His radio crackled as a message came across and I fell silent while he listened to work out if he needed to react. Behind him, the door opened yet again, and another blast of cold air swept in around my stockinged legs. We rarely got this many visitors in a day but the third drop in this morning wasn't a client either; it was Jan's partner, a short brunette woman in her late twenties. I recognized her from somewhere.

She shivered as she closed the door. 'It's starting to rain, Jan, and it's cold. I'm not waiting outside any longer so you can try to score.' Jan was looking right at me as his cheeks flushed. So he was thinking about asking me out. His partner was a bit of a cow though, calling him out like that.

I did the decent thing and moved the conversation on. 'Jennifer Lasseter. Have you met her?'

'No, why?' he asked looking relieved that I didn't react to his colleague's comment.

His partner heard me say Jennifer's name and came closer so she could join the conversation. 'Did I hear you say Jennifer Lasseter? Isn't that the woman we falsely accused and arrested for the first drowning three years ago?'

Jan nodded. 'Jane thinks the murderer leaving bodies for us to find might be a cop.'

His partner just laughed. 'Don't be ridiculous, Jan. Now, come on. We have to get going. Ask her out or don't but we have work to do. I'll be in the car.'

'Have we met?' I asked just as she turned to leave. She looked familiar but also somehow not, like I had seen her face but it had changed since.

'Yes. You saw me at the station a few days ago,' she replied. 'I was in Chief Inspector Quinn's office when you arrived on Friday.'

She went back out the door, leaving Jan and me staring at each other with a stilted silence stretching out. When he opened his mouth to speak, I jumped in quickly to beat him to it. 'I doubt I'm your type.' I said quickly.

He dropped his gaze to the floor and nodded. When he looked back up two seconds later, his usual grin was back in place. 'Worth a try. You have my number if you change your mind.' Then with a wave, he was gone too, and I was left in the office by myself.

I settled behind my desk, trying to force my brain to focus on the work I had, not the boy I fancied. There were business emails to attend to, invoices to raise and some basic accountancy to deal with since Tempest returned from France with a not-insubstantial amount of Euros.

I didn't get very far though when I saw the heading of an email near the top of my screen.

Threats. Monday, December 5th 1022hrs

THE EMAIL SUBJECT LINE read, *'You're dead meat!'* It was quite the opening gambit. Clicking the email though gave me everything I needed. The person sending the email didn't sign it to give me their name, but I didn't need it. I had their email address and could trace their IP back to where the email originated. That wouldn't even take me very long.

The body of the email contained this message:

'I told you to back off. If the fish were not enough of a deterrent, don't worry, I'm done with threats. You didn't listen so next time I see you with him, I'm going to gut you like a fish.'

A cold shiver passed down my spine. I wasn't used to being threatened. The message to back off had been a little worrying but it suggested no escalation of violence to follow. This was something else. How would I deal with it though? The first thing was to track his IP address to his actual address. Most people don't know you can do this. It doesn't even take any special skills. I simply copied it from the source code in his email, pasted it into a site called WheresthisIPaddress.com and clicked show. What popped up was a map with a pin stuck in it. As I zoomed in, I could see houses and cars and even people. It was like a Google Earth map that displayed a frozen shot from the last time the satellite passed overhead. It took a few more minutes to cross check so I had an accurate picture but by looking at a map with street names on, I knew which street the email had come from and roughly where in that street. I printed the maps off.

When I saw a chance to find the person sending the email, I got excited because I thought perhaps it was the killer, but the latest message was all about me staying away from someone. I was confused, not just because I didn't know who it was they expected me to stay away from, but also because I had thought the fish were from the killer. Now I figured they probably weren't.

The office back door banged open, scaring me half to death as I had been so focused on the idea of being gutted like a fish.

'All sorted,' said Tempest. Putting his bag down and unwinding his scarf. His two dogs came bounding through the office, bouncing off one another in their excitement. With his scarf and coat hung on the coatrack he commented that, 'It's raining hard out there now, my wipers could barely keep up.' Then he froze. 'Everything alright?'

'Um,'

'I'm going to take that as a no,' he said, starting to move again. 'If you are worrying about Karen Gilbert, don't. She doesn't blame us at all. She was happy to sign the forms so there's nothing to worry about there.' He went over to the coffee machine to switch it on then turned back to look at me again. 'That wasn't it though, was it?'

I got a grip of myself and gave it to him straight. 'I have an email that threatens me directly. It's a follow up to the message in the fish.' My reply stopped him dead in his tracks.

Coffee forgotten, he crossed the room. 'Show me, please.'

I sat back down in my chair and tapped the mouse to bring the screen back to life. Then I pushed my chair across a bit so he could lean in to read the email. As his eyes danced across the screen, I said, 'I traced the IP address already. It's a local address.'

Tempest straightened up again. 'Any idea who it is you're supposed to stop pursuing?'

I shook my head. 'I thought it was from the Biddenden Lake killer. At least, that's who I thought threw the fish yesterday.'

'Where's the address?' Tempest was already moving back to the coatrack to get his scarf. 'I think I'll do this the direct way. Would you like to come?' The question surprised me, but before I could respond, he added, 'We need to talk about your new role anyway. Pay, car, loan, stuff. We can do all that in the car.' Then he shouted for the dogs, shut them in his office where they had a bed and water and waited for me by the office back door. 'It still smells of fish in here.'

'I know,' I blushed again, but then I slipped my coat on and fluffed my hair so it fell over the collar and wasn't trapped inside. I was going out.

Pay Raise. Monday, December 5th 1039hrs

LIKE A GENTLEMAN, TEMPEST held the car door open for me to get in. I don't know if that is an automatic thing for him; I look like a woman therefore he opens doors and such, or if it was for the look of it; I look like a woman and therefore anyone looking will see him acting like a gentleman. Either way, he did it all the time and managed to switch his attitude and mannerisms seamlessly when I turned up as James instead.

Once the car was rolling, I put the postcode and road address for my gut-you-like-a-fish friend and let the car work out how to get there. The address was in Cattering, a small village on the other side of Maidstone. The satnav said it was twelve miles but a thirty-minute drive because of the tiny winding country lanes.

Tempest thumbed the call button on his steering wheel, prompting the car to ask him who he wanted to call. He shot me an embarrassed glance, then said boldly, 'Walking Penis.'

'Calling Walking Penis,' the car's automated system replied. I giggled because I knew who the walking penis was. Tempest's friend Big Ben was an Adonis with legendary pulling powers.

The call connected. 'Hey, tiny dick, what you up to?' boomed Big Ben's voice.

Tempest sighed and rolled his eyes. 'Yes, in England we say good morning. Good morning, Ben. Can you practice that?'

'Boring,' he replied.

'Ben, I'm in the car with Jane...'

'Your saucy assistant with a bit too much junk?'

This time it was my turn to roll my eyes. Tempest didn't bite though. 'We are on our way to err... have a word with someone. Are you busy?'

I heard Big Ben moving about then, talking to someone in the background. 'Not anymore. Give me the address. How soon do you need me to be there?'

'Thirty minutes? We'll hold on for you. We're just leaving Rochester actually so you might get there first if you leave now.'

'Yeah, just need to kick some girls out first. See you there.' He disconnected.

Had I heard him correctly? 'Girls?'

Tempest nodded wearily. 'Often, yes.' He paused to check a junction was clear then eased out and started talking again. 'So what do you want to do, Jane? I hired you in as an office assistant, but it is clear I would be stifling your abilities if I tried to limit you to doing just that.'

I cleared my throat. It felt like one of those conversations where one's future hangs in the balance. I needed to get this right and be sure about what it was that I did want. 'I think I want to be an investigator. I looked into the first case because we had a desperate client and you were both tied up. It was kind of the same this time but I went into it quite deliberately wondering if I could cut it as a detective. I like doing the research part of the job, but...'

'But we can hire anyone to do that,' Tempest finished my sentence. Then corrected himself. 'Well, maybe not anyone. You are significantly better at all that than I am, so I would need your help to hire in someone new. Someone with the right skills.'

'Is that what you will do? Hire in someone new?' I asked, surprised that he wanted to move so fast.

'Well,' he shrugged. 'The business is doing well. We get more enquiries all the time so not hiring a new detective would stifle the firm's development. It might as well be you that takes the role. You can transition into it as swiftly as you like, but the only thing holding you back is getting someone else in to do the admin. The research bit is something you can keep if you want.'

'You seem to have this all worked out already.'

'Ha!' he scoffed. 'I have no idea what I am doing. I'm just going with what feels right and hoping it works out. You did. So did Amanda. So did the new premises. We'll have to hot desk a little as there is no room to put a third office and no one wants to be in the storeroom.'

'Could we convert the storeroom? Put a window on the back?' I was thinking out loud, but Tempest inclined his head as he considered it.

'Maybe we could. Anyway, let's say you are now working as a detective and tomorrow will be selecting your own cases to pursue the same way Amanda and I do. Paying you as an admin assistant is no longer appropriate so I want to suggest a new package.' Then he outlined what he pays Amanda and my jaw dropped. It wasn't the basic salary that startled me, but the cut he gave her for closing cases successfully. The one element of the business he didn't let me handle was payroll. I knew what was in the bank because I dealt with the account and paid invoices in. I figured though that he kept most of the money for himself. He was doing well from the firm and got a cut of the income Amanda took from solving client's paranormal problems, but it was far from the lion's share. He was offering me the same deal. 'Does that sound fair?' he asked.

I almost wet myself in my bid to shake his hand and say yes. Suddenly my trashed Ford Fiesta wasn't much of a concern. I was going to be able to afford the repayments on a new car if I wanted one. Assuming I could close cases I reminded myself before I got too carried away.

We arrived in the street the fish-gutter's house was on and stopped short. Tempest was looking about for Big Ben's car. Then an airhorn blasted right next to my window as he screeched to a stop in his giant black car/truck thing.

'Alright losers?' Big Ben shouted down as he hung out his open window. I had a hand to my heart as I prayed it would restart soon.

'He is such a delight,' muttered Tempest as he opened his door. Big Ben swung his big car around in front of Tempest's and parked, leaping energetically down to the pavement to make the beast rock side to side on its suspension.

Once all three of us were on the street, Tempest asked, 'You said, the person should be home?'

'Their IP was live and being used when I checked. They are either on a day off or they work from home.'

Big Ben cracked his knuckles and patted his groin, giving his junk a quick feel. 'Yup, both ready for action. Is it a girl or a boy we are here to annoy?'

I shrugged. 'I traced an IP address.'

That didn't do it for Big Ben though. 'So, that means...'

I rolled my eyes yet again. 'I can't tell. All I know is there is a computer in that house that was used to send me a threatening message.'

Big Ben rolled his shoulders and hunched over into a boxer's pose. 'Let's find out then.'

'Hold up,' Tempest grabbed his arm. 'We are going to be polite. At least until it is time to stop being polite. If you wish to take over at that point, you may do so.'

We didn't get that far though because the door of the house we were standing outside of was yanked open and a short man with a baseball bat and an aggressive expression appeared. 'I warned you!' he roared. 'I warned you to stay away from him. That's all you had to do and instead you come here and you bring muscle with you. Am I supposed to be intimidated?'

Big Ben, Tempest and I all looked at each other. 'Um, yes?' said Big Ben. 'We are fairly scary. Well, I am anyway. Tempest not so much.'

'Be quiet, knob jockey,' Tempest hissed. Then he addressed the irritated man, 'Sir, I must request that you put down the bat so we can calmly discuss your need to threaten my colleague.'

The man said something rather colourful in response that could be shortened to a firm no. What I wanted to know was who it was I was supposed to be staying away from. I didn't get to ask though because the crazy man attacked us.

If I hadn't been so startled by his aggression, I might have been entertained. As I took a pace back, my feet moving themselves as instinct took over, Big Ben and Tempest stepped forward. The man had the bat above his head and was running across his front lawn screaming, 'Aaaarrrrghhh!' as loud as he could manage.

Nonchalantly, as if they were being charged by an angry hamster, Big Ben asked, 'You or me?'

Tempest shrugged. 'Me? Then you can finish?'

Big Ben bowed theatrically at Tempest, turned toward the attacker and said, 'Sure.' Then several things happened really quickly. The guys both took a step to the side, each one going a different direction so the man's attention was split, then as he glanced at Big Ben, Tempest darted back in and the man took a wild swing at the sudden threat. Tempest continued his motion though, carrying onward toward the man so that as the man swung his bat, Tempest was inside the man's personal space and at the fulcrum of the swing where it had no power.

He plucked the bat from his surprised grasp and Big Ben thumped him on top of his head with one meaty fist. The man dropped to the floor with both hands on his head to shield it from further injury.

It was like watching a choreographed dance.

Tempest threw the bat back towards the man's house. 'Now then, what say you we have a more dignified chat?'

He looked kind of pathetic and harmless now that he was unarmed and on the grass, so I crouched down to bring myself closer to his eyeline. 'Who is it you are trying to get me to stay away from?' I asked.

'What?'

'You threatened me and demanded I stay away from someone. I don't know who you are talking about. I'm not involved with anyone.'

'You're not?' His face bore a perplexed expression. 'But I've seen you with him.'

'Who?' I demanded with a large helping of impatience.

'Jan Van Doorn. He's my boyfriend. Was my boyfriend,' he corrected himself. 'We split up a few weeks back. I need him back. I need him to see how much I love him...'

I wasn't listening anymore; Jan was gay. How had I not known? Jan was gay and that changed everything. He was trying to ask me out earlier which must mean that he knows I'm not a girl. And I told him I'm not his type. Dammit.

I began to walk back to the car. 'Err, Jane,' called Tempest, his voice causing me to stop and turn around again. 'Are we done here?'

'I thought he was connected to the Biddenden Lake murders. He's not, so I guess I have no interest in him.'

On the ground still, the man spluttered, his ire rising at my dismissal. As he tried to get up though, Big Ben moved slightly and put a large foot on the man's hand. 'You're not thinking of doing something rash, are you, sir?' asked Tempest. 'Gutting my colleague like a fish for instance.'

He mumbled something and when prompted to speak a little louder, he shouted, 'No!' Then there was an uncomfortable interlude where Tempest insisted the man apologise and then recorded him admitting his crime, stating his name and address and promising to never contact me or any member of Blue Moon again.

I was glad to be back in Tempest's car when it was done. It was another dead-end lead though. Three cops were dead, and I was no nearer to working out who was to blame.

Half the day was gone and there was work waiting for me back at the office. In the quiet of the car on the ride back to Rochester, I thought about the new position Tempest had offered me. He had no plan to look into the Biddenden Lake case; we had no client now that CI Quinn had pulled the plug on our contract and was sure the police would work it out for themselves. His offer though allowed me to choose my own cases. If I picked a non-paying one and worked on it in my own time, I was sure he would not object.

I wasn't done with the swamp monster yet.

A Clue in a Puddle. Monday, December 5th 1547hrs

THE AFTERNOON SLIPPED BY in a blur, the minutes merging into each other as I performed routine tasks and helped Amanda with some basic research. She had what appeared to be a case on the coast where a biker gang wanted to hire us. Two of their gang members had been killed, found dead with bite marks the local coroner had confirmed to contain wolf saliva.

They were pointing the finger at a new gang who called themselves the Herne Bay Howlers. The Howlers had a howling wolf as their gang symbol. Amanda asked if I could pull together some basic information on the parties involved and that had eaten up a couple of hours.

The work seemed mundane now though. What had been interesting last week, was now a challenge to focus on because I knew there was something more exciting I could be doing. I caught myself daydreaming more than once, my attention drifting off to consider the swamp monster case. Should I pursue it? Should I leave it alone?

Just as I pressed send on the file to get it to Amanda, my stomach gurgled; I had skipped lunch. From her office, Amanda called out, 'Thanks, Jane.' But she didn't look up to see me give her a thumbs up.

The next task on my list was to send the reply to Lord Hale's invitation. There was a RSVP email address to which I was expected to send a list of attendees. Tempest's list included his parents, Jagjit and Alice, Big Ben and Patience and both he and Amanda. He asked me if I wanted to attend with Simon but realized his mistake almost before the words left his mouth. He then apologized unnecessarily several times while I assured him it was okay.

With that task complete, my stomach reminded me of its emptiness. I needed to eat something. The move meant the snacks I would normally have in the fridge to make lunch with were still in the fridge at Simon's house and I wasn't getting them back. I could do some shopping to get a few bits into gran's cupboards later. Right now, though, I needed a sandwich.

Outside, the rain had moved on and the pavement on the pedestrianized High Street was beginning to dry. Heading to a sandwich shop along the street, I found myself behind a woman with two little girls. They were twins and perhaps eight or nine years old and they were squabbling as kids do. The mother was losing her rag at them which was having no effect as the pair continued to fight. As they drew level with a large puddle, one shoved the other into it. Both were wearing wellington boots so getting their shoes wet was no issue at all but the one in the puddle took offense and chased after her sister, both of them running through the next puddle.

I stopped walking. On the pavement in front of me was the answer to the whole damned swamp monster case. How had no one considered it. I felt my heart thump in my chest, a wave of exhilaration sweeping through me like adrenalin.

Despite my heeled boots, I ran back to the office. Neither Tempest nor Amanda were there but I didn't need them, I wasn't going to tackle the killer or get into a fight with anyone. I was going to do some research, prove to myself what I thought I knew and then contact the police. Chief Inspector Quinn might be a person I was never going to like but if I was right, then he was about to get killed by the same people that had killed the previous three victims and Ian Dexter.

It was the footprints. The footprints; the fact that the only footprints at the scene were those of Ian Dexter and Jennifer Lasseter was the key argument used by her lawyer to ensure her release. It was also erroneous. What they were looking at were three sets of footprints, but two of them were wearing the same shoe and weighed roughly the same so had caused the same depth of impression.

That had to be it. But the answer also threw up a stack of new questions. Jennifer Lasseter was guilty, that was the instant conclusion I could draw. Her footprints were at the scene three years ago and she was the only one that saw the supposed swamp monster. She had an accomplice at the time, most likely another woman given the shoe size, but it could be a small man. Solving that crime did not necessarily solve the current spate of murders though. There were no footprints found near the bodies, no entry point found where the killers had placed the bodies in the water, and they could tell they had drowned at the lake from the water found in their lungs.

My computer booted into life as I settled into the chair. I hadn't bothered to take my coat off; I didn't think this was going to take very long. Now that I could see that Jennifer was guilty, I thought I knew where to find the accomplice as well.

In Jennifer's social media pages, there were photographs going back to her childhood. My earlier research skimmed through them, but something had stuck with me. It didn't mean anything at the time, but it lay dormant in my brain until it was triggered by something else. I didn't know what it was until now, but as I clicked through to find the image set I wanted, the feeling of dread came back.

Michelle the cop, the one who was partnering Jan was a childhood friend of Jennifer's. I stared at pictures of the two of them together and knew I had it right. Someone had leaked the swamp monster picture and someone had helped Jennifer murder her boyfriend in a manner that the police wouldn't be able to prove. She was the right height and the right weight, and she had been involved in the original case. Unable to take my eyes off the screen, my hand fumbled for my phone and knocked it off the edge of the desk. Too late, I dived after it, only to see it bounce off the edge of the bin and shoot across the floor. The noise it made as it hit the tile did not fill me with confidence so it was no shock when I turned it over to find the screen dead.

Uttering a few choice words of frustration, I threw the dead phone into my handbag and ran to the back door. I couldn't call the chief inspector, but the drive there would only take me ten to fifteen minutes at this time of day. I could show him the evidence myself.

Incredibly I was in the carpark and rooting around in my bag for my keys before I remembered that my car was dead. I skidded to a halt, slapping myself on the forehead.

What was I going to do now? Use the office phone instead of your mobile? Cursing myself for my stupidity, I turned to go back inside.

Then, an odd little giggle stopped me short. I couldn't see the person who made the noise, they were obscured by the corner of the building. A sense of movement to my right was all I got as a warning before a burst of pain exploded in my skull. Someone had hit me though I didn't know with what and I was falling, an odd sensation of the ground coming up to meet me as my consciousness was replaced by a fuzzy feeling of blackness.

Then, just as my vision shut down, that odd little giggle again.

Swamp Monster. Monday, December 5th, no idea what time.

I COULDN'T WORK OUT if I was having a dream or not. Trying to focus on what I could see didn't make any sense, the images wouldn't align properly and that made me question whether I was asleep. Then pain hit me, flashing behind my eyes and forcing me to close them again.

'Oh, my, lord,' I whispered to myself. There were strip lights above me, bright bars of blinding white light that bored into my eyeballs to set my brain on fire when I opened my eyelids. I tried to roll over, but my limbs didn't want to respond to my commands.

'Don't bother,' said a familiar woman's voice to the accompaniment of a giggle. Where did I know the voice from? Oh, yeah. Outside the office, just before someone hit me over the head, the odd little laugh. It sounded deranged. Carefully, slowly, I opened my eyes just a fraction so I could squint between my mostly closed lashes to see where I was. There wasn't much to see.

The cold penetrating my right side was coming from a concrete floor. I was lying on it with nothing to separate me from the freezing stone. I tried to move again but my limbs didn't feel like they were connected to my body or my brain didn't feel like it was connected to anything. Something like that. Speaking wasn't much better. I could move my tongue, but my teeth felt unfamiliar in my mouth and the words were garbled. 'Where am I?' I asked the unseen person, though I wasn't sure they would understand the noises I made.

Then hands grabbed my shoulders to roll me over and pull me across the concrete. I caught a glimpse of the person but there was something wrong with my eyes because it didn't look like a person. As they stepped back, I learned that my eyes were not playing tricks on me. I was, in fact, being manhandled by the swamp monster.

'You'll want to watch this part,' it said. Tempest likes to say that it is always some idiot in a costume when actually it has regularly proven in the past to be several other things instead. Today though, he would have been bang on the money.

It wasn't even a good suit. I could even go as far as to describe it as rubbish. I could see a pair of feet sticking out the bottom of the giant monster feet; they were wearing a pair of Adidas hightop running shoes. It looked rubbery and fake and generally unconvincing. The hands of the monster suit were not articulated. Rather, they were big floppery things that articulated at the wrist to fold out of the way so the person in the suit could stick their own hands out. Don't get me started on the head piece.

I was having trouble keeping my head up though, it lolled forward a bit so I needed to look out of the top of my eyes, almost staring through my eyebrows to look in front of me. The monster was dragging something across the floor, but I couldn't quite see what it was.

'What did you give me?' I asked. Speaking made my head burst with pain again so I didn't repeat it even though it sounded wrong in my ears.

'Did you catch that?' a new voice asked the monster. Both voices were female and definitely familiar. I was struggling to put a face to either though. Then it said, 'Oh, it can't see. Give me a second.' Hands clamped my head, making it pound once more as she tilted my head up and used the wall to hold it in place. 'That's better.'

Then she crouched in front of me and I saw who my captor was. 'Hello, Jennifer,' I tried.

'Dude, you are making no sense at all. How much did you give her?' she asked over her shoulder while continuing to look in my eyes.

'The same amount we gave everyone else,' came a reply from somewhere.

'But dude she's half the size.' Then the giggle again.

In response Jennifer got a noise that sounded like Michelle couldn't give a damn. Jennifer checked my head wasn't going to move then stood up. As she moved, I discovered she had been blocking the view beyond with her body. Now, sitting opposite me I saw Chief Inspector Quinn. He was naked from the waist up and clearly half frozen from the same cold I felt. Oddly he had gloves on his hands which triggered me to think about mine. I shifted my eyes downward. Though I felt groggy and sick, I could move my eyeballs around. I looked at my hands; I had gloves on. They were not mine. I looked back at Chief Inspector Quinn. He looked at me but didn't say anything. He wasn't bound but he wasn't trying to resist either so whatever they had given me, they must have given him as well. Somewhere inside my fog-filled brain, I knew what it was. I just couldn't name it.

It had been the chief inspector the monster had been dragging across the floor and a spark connected inside my head. 'Michelle.'

'I think she just said your name,' said Jennifer.

'Who cares?' replied the monster. 'And I told you; it's a guy not a girl.'

'Looks like a girl,' Jennifer argued.

'Check the undercarriage if you don't believe me.'

'Eww, no thanks.'

Then the monster came into view again and approached me. I couldn't tilt my head up to see it and couldn't get my eyes to look up at an acute enough angle to see its face, but I guess Michelle knew that because she came down to my level. Her face was masked inside the monster suit which covered all of her hair and came under her chin to cover her throat. She studied me for a moment, staring at me as if curious. Then she slapped me. As hard as she could using

149

the back of her right hand against my left cheekbone and as my head exploded in pain, I registered the blow to my cheek as well.

'That was just to make sure you were paying attention,' she said with a little laugh. 'You see, each time we kill one of the guys,' she said the guys with speech mark finger held aloft. 'We tell them why. It's just our thing. It's such a wonderful cliché to reveal the master plan that we felt it would be gauche to not follow tradition. In a moment, the chief inspector is going to receive injuries much akin to those inflicted on the previous victims. The bites, the bruising. Not the worst bites though, the ones where we tear off bits of flesh, we save those for in the water just before we drown them. They can't be post-mortem, you see. The coroner would know the difference.' She looked into my panicked eyes and raised a hand to stroke my hair. 'Don't worry, you'll get to watch us torture him. In fact, maybe we should get on with it. I can tell you the rest while we get creative.'

Michelle gave my cheek one last, tender pat, then left me propped against the wall and disappeared from sight. When she returned a few seconds later she had a set of teeth in her hands. No, that's wrong. She had a pair of jaws with teeth in them. When she saw me staring, she said, 'You like these? I picked them up on eBay. I think they might have been a movie prop from some old sci-fi horror movie or something. I'm not sure they were designed for cutting flesh per se, but they sharpened up real good.'

Then she thrust them at Chief Inspector Quinn's back and snapped them closed on his flesh. I had to watch as he screamed in pain, the almost inhuman noise escaping his lips despite bracing himself for it.

Then, from the left, Jennifer came running with something in her hands and swung it like a bat. Only once it struck home and she stepped back did I see what it was; a plastic monster hand. That was how the bruises had come to be on the victims. Just as CI Quinn recoiled from the blow, Michelle bit into his shoulder with the teeth again.

I had to watch while they went at him for what felt like ten minutes but was probably no more than two. Quinn kept falling over and they kept sitting him back up. They got bored with that after a while though and just let him flop forward while they continued to attack him.

It was awful. And I could only assume they were making me watch because I was next.

Jennifer kept taking a run up to deliver her blows and was slightly out of breath when she smiled at me and dropped the tool on the floor. 'Were you expecting the same?' she gave me the chance to reply then giggled because she knew I couldn't. 'We can't mess with the ritual. The guilty ones get drowned by the swamp monster. It's a fun name, isn't it? The press are so inventive.' I could tell she was being sarcastic but there was nothing I could do about it. 'Anyway, you will be spared all of that fun, we're just going to strangle you and dump your body. You dress like a slut and you're a freak, a transsexual, transgender...' she waved a hand in my direction. 'I don't even care what you are; it's weird. So, we decided we could leave your body and make it look like you were into some weird sex game and it went too far. Michelle's idea of course. She sees so much of this stuff so can just replicate something she read about in another county.'

Jennifer giggled again and mimed hearing me ask her a question. 'What's that? Why? Why are we killing all the nice policemen?' As she screamed her answer, she ran at Chief Inspector Quinn's inert form and kicked him hard in his exposed ribs. 'Because they deserve it. Just like Ian deserved it. He beat me, you know?' Jennifer shoved her face back in front of mine. 'He beat me and put me in hospital and told me I could never leave him. So I asked Michelle how I could kill him in a way that no one would ever tie it to me. She helped me get rid of that pig.' Another giggle escaped her lips. 'I wanted to take pictures when Michelle held him under. His face was such a picture; he couldn't believe it. He couldn't believe the woman he had degraded and beaten could ever rise against him. But I got to watch the air in his lungs run out and the light fade from his eyes. It's a memory I will cherish forever.' She finished with another giggle.

'We need to get moving,' echoed Michelle's voice from somewhere unseen.

'Oops,' Jennifer giggled again. 'Just enough time left to finish the story though, I think. You must be wondering why we went back to killing recently. It's addictive. That's why. I wanted to do it again ever since the first time. The raw power of it. Ooooh!' She grinned and wriggled with her eyes closed like she was having an orgasm. 'It took a while to talk Michelle into it, but I knew who

I wanted to target; those pigs that made me feel guilty about killing Ian. They had me in a cell for weeks, accusing me, trying to get me to admit that I did it. Trying to prove I could have manhandled that enormous brute into the water by myself. They deserve it as much as he did, and Quinn was their leader.' She ran and kicked him again, twice for good measure. 'I told you I didn't do it. He was so smug and knowing, like he knew it was me and it was only a matter of time until he worked out how. Well, I showed them. He's the last one. Then we have to find some new targets.'

'No,' snapped Michelle. 'I told you, this is the end of it. I agreed to this because they are all misogynistic pigs. They treated me as if I was there to bring them tea. Quinn was the worst; he stole my ideas and passed them off as his own. He has to be the last one. If we keep going, they will work out that we are putting them into the lake via a feeding river and will catch us. Now, come on, we have to go.'

'Yes, Michelle,' Jennifer replied dutifully, then leaned in close so she could whisper to me. 'She'll come around. This is too much fun to give up.'

Still drugged, I watched as they lifted the chief inspector into the boot of an old Volvo. They took no care at all, swinging his body and then releasing it so he struck his head on the frame of the car and landed with a hard thump. An arm hung out and I thought Jennifer was going to slam the boot lid down on it until Michelle shoved it in at the last moment.

Then I realised that in order to have watched them load the car, I had to have turned my head. I had managed to turn my head. Did that mean the drugs were wearing off? I turned it back as I saw them come for me. Roughly grabbed under my arms and around my ankles, they carried me to a different car I hadn't seen. It was in front of the Volvo, its boot open again to receive me. Michelle, who was holding my arms, dumped me on the floor though.

'What's happening?' asked Jennifer.

'I need to get this stupid monster suit off. I can't drive in it and we need to gag this one. She'll get her voice back before her body starts to work and I don't want her yelling in the boot to draw attention.'

Jennifer dropped my feet. 'I don't see why you don't just up the dose. Then you wouldn't run the risk of them coming around.'

Michelle was behind me somewhere, struggling with the costume and swearing in her efforts to get it off. 'How many times have I told you this? If the drug is too potent, the coroner will find it when he does the autopsy. It needs to be almost out of the person's system when we kill them.'

Jennifer sighed. 'Yes, Michelle.' Then she giggled as Michelle grabbed my head to force a silk scarf between my teeth. She yanked it roughly as she tied it behind my head, little flashes of light dancing in front of my eyes from the pain.

'Now she's ready,' announced Michelle and they picked me up again, threw me into the boot of the car and slammed it shut. All was dark.

Outside, I could hear their muffled voices. Then they fell silent and I heard an engine start up. It must be the Volvo because it sounded distant. Then the engine of the car I was in rumbled to life. I heard the parking brake being released and suddenly I was moving. I had no idea where I was going but I knew they planned to kill me.

I had to get control of my body and put up a fight when they tried to get me out again. They wouldn't be expecting it, but though I could now move my head from side to side, that was all I had. I could just about manage to flop my arms a bit.

I was going to die and there would be nothing I could do about it as the life was squeezed out of me.

Familiar Territory. Monday, December 5th unsure of time

TRACKING WHERE I MIGHT be or how long I had been in the boot of the car proved impossible. I had no idea where I was when they put me in the car or how long had passed since they took me. All I knew was they intended to kill me when the car reached its destination. The car stopped occasionally, at junctions or for traffic lights, I assumed, but I heard no other car noises around me and no light penetrated the boot so it either had a tight seal, or the lack of traffic noise meant it was the middle of the night.

This was bad because it meant no one would be looking for me. Probably not even gran. Gran would assume I had gone out or was working late. She most likely planned to tell me off for not calling but wouldn't think to report my absence until I failed to show the next evening.

When I felt the car take a slow right turn and begin bumping along uneven ground, I knew we had to be getting close to where they were taking me. Try as I might, I still couldn't get my limbs under control. They were better than they were, and I would be able to put up some kind of defense, but it wouldn't be much.

The car stopped with a final lurch and unwanted terror gripped me when the engine shut down.

Silence. Nothing but the sound of my own labored breathing until I heard a car door open a moment later. The girls were being stealthy in their movements, quietly pushing the doors closed instead of slamming them. Then there was noise right next to my ear and the boot opened once more.

It was full dark out and we were under a canopy of trees. Michelle and Jennifer were distinguishable only by the moonlight filtering down between the branches. They both reached in to grab me, Michelle going for my arms as Jennifer tried to grab my legs. I was ready for them though, pushing off the floor of the boot with my shoulders as I flailed my arms and legs to block them. I shouted to get them away or attract attention but it just came out as a, 'Blaaargh,' noise because of the tight gag in my mouth.

They both burst out laughing. 'That was pathetic,' giggled Jennifer. Then she reached behind her back to pull a kitchen knife from somewhere. Light glinted off the blade as she held it up. Exchanging her smile for a sneer, she pointed the knife at me. 'Do it again and part of your death by weird sex game will include you getting feminized.'

'She means it,' added Michelle. 'You should have heeded the warnings. I really thought that burning your car and your girlfriend's house would deter you. Actually, the intention was to kill you, but I figured we might as well burn the car as well because then if you did survive, you might get the message. Now, I'm going to reach in and grab your arms. If you resist, Jennifer is going to stab you in the balls. Do you understand?'

I nodded.

'I couldn't see that. Did you just nod?' asked Michelle. 'It's dark here, man. Look, I'm reaching in, behave or get stabbed; the choice is yours.'

I knew what I needed to do. I needed to get their flesh under my skin so a crime lab would be able to find it and identify my killers. I needed to bite them or scratch them or something, but Michelle was too clever for that. The gloves on my hands prevented me from scratching them at all and the gag in my mouth stopped me from talking but also provided a nice accessory for their sex game gone wrong ending.

As Michelle levered me out of the boot and sat me on the lip, she asked. 'Can you walk?'

Jennifer had the knife pressed hard against my ribs and a hand hooked around my neck so she had leverage to stick me with it if I tried to wriggle free. I tried to force my brain to come up with a way I could escape. Maybe shove one against the other and run for it? Twist away and grab for the knife so I had a weapon I could use? Scenario after scenario ran through my head but they all seemed improbable or impossible and though I could stand, it was all I could manage to stumble forward with both women holding me upright.

Michelle let go with one hand so she could look at her watch. I caught a glimpse: It was only just after eight-thirty, far earlier than I thought. She tutted. 'When we get him in place, you need to get back to the car and get to the drop off point. I'll catch up with you. We lost too much time dealing with this one. If I am late for shift at ten it will be questioned.'

'But I want to see you strangle her,' whined Jennifer.

'It's a him not a her and you can't. We don't have time.'

Huffily, Jennifer argued, 'Then let me strangle her or him or whatever it is, and you take Quinn to the lake.'

Michelle suddenly stopped walking, her grip on my arm stopping me too. 'We stick with the plan, Jennifer.' Michelle's tone would take no argument.

Her psychotic friend backed down. 'Okay, Michelle. There's no need to get bossy. Can I cut him before I go though? Maybe circumcise him a bit?' she asked with another giggle.

'No,' hissed Michelle. 'You should go back to the car. We are close enough. I'm going to do it just down there by the bridge.' When Jennifer didn't let go of me, she said, 'Now, Jennifer,' in her insistent tone.

Jennifer's grip on me loosened and then let go. With a final whine about wanting to kill me, she did as Michelle ordered.

'This is a popular dogging spot. We often catch people here doing things they shouldn't because it leads to the housing estate from the High Street where there are pubs. It's a Tuesday night though and too early for doggers to be out.'

Stumbling along the dirt path, I hadn't questioned where we were because it made no difference. Now though, as we rounded the final bend, I saw the bridge ahead of me and knew exactly where I was.

I was in West Kinglsey park and that was Arthur's bridge. I wanted to cry at the irony of my life. If I hadn't taken the time to talk Arthur into reforming, he might be under there now, ready to jump out on anyone that came near. I was freezing cold, ready to wet myself with fright and though I had solved the case and found the killers, I hadn't done so soon enough to prevent them finishing their killing spree and taking me out for good measure. Would anyone catch them now?

Michelle switched her grip on my arm as she turned me around to place the bridge behind us. Then yanked the belt even tighter around my throat. Then she kicked the back of my knees so I crashed down into the mud of the path on all fours. She was behind me with a knee against my back and both hands on the belt. There wasn't a thing I could do as I felt the belt tighten and sparkles began to dance in front of my eyes. Flailing ineffectually at the wide belt, the gloves ensured I could get no purchase.

Sir Arthur. Monday, December 5th 2042hrs

MICHELLE DIDN'T EVEN BOTHER to speak. It was just a task to get done so she could move on. Like washing up or doing the ironing: Kill annoying private detective, drown chief inspector, go to work.

'What the...?' Michelle's grip faltered and then failed and oxygen flooded into my lungs as I took a ragged breath in.

'Get off my bridge!'

It was Arthur! The damned fool had lied about giving up his life as an ogre. I had one hand in the mud as I tried to pull the glove off my right hand with my teeth. It wouldn't come but the belt was loose enough for me to breathe so, I clambered onto wobbly feet to see where he was.

Michelle screamed a banshee war cry and swiped at the huge man with a knife. Like Jennifer she had brought a kitchen knife with her but it wasn't going to do her much good against Arthur the ogre.

They were down by the bridge, light from the moon illuminating the scene perfectly as Michelle switched grip and lunged again. Filled with hope that I might live, I had to distract her attention to give him an opening.

I tore the gag off and shouted, 'Hey!' it still didn't sound right but she glanced my way and Arthur punched her in the face. I knew how big his hands were; it must have been like getting hit in the face with a small building. She didn't just go down; she flew backward six feet first to land in the bushes and nettles next to the river.

Arthur took a step back which brought him up against the stonework of the bridge. He was holding his right side with one hand. 'Arthur, are you alright? Did she hurt you?'

'It's Sir Arthur, if you please, Lady Jane,' he chided, somehow convincing himself that he was an ogre and a knight. 'Fear not, though, sweet child, tis not much more than a stitch in my side from the unexpected effort. I should worry more whether you are alright. That lady appeared to intend you harm.'

'She was trying to strangle the life out of me, Sir Arthur.' I rubbed my throat. She hadn't been far from success when he interrupted her. 'Oh, lord!'

'What is it, my dear? Are you hurt?'

Whether it was lack of oxygen making it to my brain or something else, I had forgotten about Chief Inspector Quinn. 'Do you have a phone with you?'

'No, m'lady. That would be completely inappropriate for hiding beneath a bridge.' Of course he didn't have a phone, he was penniless.

'Then we have to go. She has an accomplice and she is going to kill someone else if we don't stop her.'

'There's not a moment to waste then. Let us away from this place. Um, what do we do with this one?' Sir Arthur was nudging Michelle's foot with his own. 'I think I knocked her out.'

I should think he did. 'We have to take her with us. Can you carry her?'

Leaving Michelle for a moment, Sir Arthur came to where I had found a spot to lean against a tree. 'Are you sure that you can walk, Lady Jane?' You look unsteady on your feet.

He was right. I was still unsteady. I pushed myself upright though. 'I can make it. We need to get back along this path. Her car is there, and we can take that. I think I know where we need to go.'

'I'll get the young lady then.' Sir Arthur went back for Michelle as I began wobbling along the path. Time was of the essence but when I tried to go a little faster, I stumbled and fell to my knees.

I didn't stay there though, a giant arm scooped me into the air and Sir Arthur had me balanced on his right arm. I looked over his shoulder to find that he had Michelle by her right hand and was dragging her back along the path like a toddler with a teddy bear.

'There's her car,' I pointed. It was the first time I had seen it properly. When they threw me in the boot, I had no idea nor concern what sort of car it was. Now I could see it was a Vauxhall Astra.

Sir Arthur tutted. 'Oh no. No, this won't do at all.'

'I'm sorry?'

'This car. It has no style. No presence.'

'It's what we've got,' I pointed out, levering myself out of his arms so I could search Michelle for her keys. As I patted her down, I saw how dumb my drug addled brain was. I should have searched her for a phone the first chance I got. A phone would have meant I could call Tempest or Amanda or gran and most definitely the police.

The keys weren't on her though and neither was her phone. I checked the car to find it locked. Under the wheel arches and all other obvious hiding places yielded the same result: No keys and staring through the windshield I could see her phone sitting on the center console.

I swore. 'Lady Jane,' Sir Arthur chided. 'Such language is unbecoming of a young lady. If I may though, I believe I can present an alternative solution.'

'I'm all ears?'

'Such a strange expression. My abode is not far from here. I have cars there that we may avail ourselves to.'

'You have a car?' I asked, frowning. 'Last week you were a tramp. Now you have a car?'

Sir Arthur's reply was as odd as the rest of him. 'I am Sir Arthur Chestwick-Fontneau. I have everything.'

I flapped my arms in frustration. It wasn't like I had a choice about things. 'Do you have a phone there as well?' I asked as I started along the path again.

'Yes, m'lady. Are you recovered? You are walking more steadily now.' He was right, my legs felt stronger and my head clearer. No doubt, this was deliberate on the girls' part because they wanted the Rohypnol to be untraceable. Time it so the drug is just wearing off at the time of death and the coroner won't be able to prove it was ever there.

To Sir Arthur's question, I replied, 'Yes, we should hurry.'

And hurry we did, just about reaching a jog as we exited the woods and came onto the pavement. Sir Arthur and I had been on this exact spot just a few days ago when I took him for cake and let him unload his woes. How had I got from there to here?

'Where to?' I asked. Now that we were out of the woods, I had no idea which direction his house might be in.

'Just across the road, m'lady.' He pointed across the street.

I turned and looked, raised my eyebrows and turned back to look at his face. 'You've got to be kidding me.'

With Michelle tucked under his arm like a rag doll, he crossed the road and pushed open the huge wrought iron gate. 'Not one bit, my dear. This is the family home.'

As I followed him in, I saw the crest on the gate. It was the same one he wore on his blazer. 'You've got to be kidding me.' The words escaped in a hushed breath of wonder as I looked up at the giant house. I had driven by it many times without ever looking at it. It was just another grand house and there were lots of them about. 'But, but, you dress like you're homeless and you live under a bridge.'

'I don't live under the bridge, dear lady. I merely choose to reenact one of my father's fondest stories.'

'Your father?' I repeated, not following what he was telling me.

'Yes, he's the chap that wrote the *Ogre Under the Bridge*. He observed me playing with my friends one day when I was but a boy. He conjured the story right there and then. Of course he was already a successful author at the time but it became his best-seller.' Arthur reached the enormous oak front door and pushed it open. As he got inside, he yelled a single word, 'Bates!'

Standing behind him and feeling utterly bewildered, I watched as he settled Michelle on the tiled floor. A man in his forties wearing a pink apron over a white shirt and black trousers came through a door to our right. He had pink marigold gloves on his hands. He said, 'Good evening, Sir Arthur.'

'This is Bates, my valet,' Sir Arthur explained. 'Bates, I need you to look after this young lady and call the police. She has been rather naughty.'

'Very good, sir. Will you be wanting supper?'

'I have to go out again. I need my phone, can you fetch a jacket for Lady Jane, please and fetch the keys for the Aston Martin? I feel that speed will be a virtue tonight.'

'Very good, sir. In which order would you like these tasks performed, sir?' asked Bates, his tone bored.'

'Use your common sense, man,' sighed Sir Arthur. 'The girl is clearly unconscious, Lady Jane is clearly cold, and I am clearly getting impatient. Give me the car keys and the phone, fetch the damned jacket and then call the police.' As Bates slowly scurried away at a butler's unhurried pace, a feat which was remarkable to watch, Sir Arthur put a hand to his side again.

'Are you alright, Sir Arthur,' I asked moving to see if he was hurt.

'It's nothing but a scratch, my dear. Nothing to worry about. Ah, here is Bates with the keys.' Bates had taken the time to fetch a silver tray and placed a purple felt cloth over it so he could present the keys to the master of the house. Sir Arthur snatched them up, knocking the cloth to the floor. 'Meet me outside with that jacket, and for goodness sake, hurry, man.'

Sir Arthur grabbed my hand and we ran from the house. I had no idea where we were going but across a gravel drive we came to another building. It was brick-built with a low roof. Once inside the lights came on automatically, the blinking strobes lighting up car after car after car as they stretched into the distance. 'My father had a thing for cars. I can't say I share it, but they come in handy occasionally.'

Right at the front, for we had entered from the back, was a low-slung dark grey Aston Martin. It was an older model, something from the eighties I thought but it was sleek and powerful looking.

It wasn't locked, so as Sir Arthur swung behind the wheel, I scampered around to the passenger side and slid in. The brutish engine roared to life instantly as the garage door swung open before us. Then we were going, Sir Arthur aiming the car at his butler then away at the last second so he could snag the jacket through his window as we passed. 'Here you are, my dear. I'll get the heaters on as well. Now where are we going?'

Rescue. Monday, December 5th 2112hrs

THE CAR WAS AN incredible piece of machinery but I didn't have much chance to appreciate it because I was on the phone. Sir Arthur handed it to me so I could use it after explaining that the mobile phone hadn't been invented when the car was made. The first call I made was to Tempest. I remembered his number but when I got no answer I was stuck because I hadn't memorized any other numbers. I wanted to call Jan but since I couldn't I dialed three nines and waited for the call to connect.

I got the operator and then got the police dispatch line at which point I started spewing information as fast as I could.

The dispatcher stopped me. 'You're going to have to slow down, caller. Let's start with your name.'

Gritting my teeth, I said. 'This is Jane Butterworth. You don't have time to be asking questions. Chief Inspector Quinn from the Maidstone branch of Kent Police has been kidnapped and is about to be murdered unless you stick a rocket up your arse and get moving.'

'Caller, are you threatening to kill someone?' the dispatcher asked, the woman's tone at least getting a little more excited now.

This was going to take too long. I switched tack. 'Is Patience Woods there? I need to speak to her, right now.'

'Caller...'

'GIVE ME PATIENCE WOODS NOW!' I bellowed.

There was a click and a new voice came on the line, 'Hello, caller...'

Hearing a familiar voice, I interrupted once again, 'Patience, this is Jane the crossdresser.' I figured I might as well just say it and short cut the bit where I had to explain who I was.

'Oh, hey girlfriend. What'cha calling for?'

'I know who the Biddenden Lake murderer is. She has Chief Inspector Quinn and she's about to kill him.' I heard her mumble something that sounded like *hooray*, but I pressed on. 'I'm on my way there now but I need back up.'

Getting into gear, I heard Patience start shouting at people in the dispatch room. A second later she was back in my ear. 'Sugar, there's already cops at Biddenden Lake. They're hiding out in case the killer shows up at any point.'

'She's not putting them in the lake. They're going into one of the feeder rivers that flows into it. That's why there are no footprints or marks around the lake to show how the bodies are getting into the water.'

'Where do I need to send the cars, sugar?'

I opened my mouth to tell her but shut it again. I was only guessing that I knew where Jennifer was going, I wasn't certain and I had no idea how long she would wait for Michelle to arrive before drowning him herself. If, like me, the Rohypnol was wearing off, the chief inspector would be able to move and fight so I doubted she would hang around long.

'The cars, sugar. Where do I need to send them?' Patience prompted me when I didn't speak.

'Dammit, I'm not sure. Somewhere west of Biddenden Lake.' There was more than one river feeding the lake and there had to be plenty of points where a body could be pushed in. They wouldn't want to carry it far though! 'Patience, can you pull up a map of the area? We need to look for points where the road runs close to the water. That's where they will be.'

'Sure thing, sugar. Hold on a moment now.' I could hear other voices around her; one of their own was in trouble and they were pulling together. She said something to someone, the sound of her voice muffled as if she put her hand on the microphone before speaking to them. 'I have a map, girl. There's three rivers though.'

'It has to be wide enough to carry a man's body down and into the lake.'

'Okay well that rules out that one,' she replied.

I thought some more. 'Do any of them have locks?'

'Wow, yeah. Good call. If we rule out the Geer River, it only leaves one, so let's look at the Tike.' There was discussion at the other end, and I had a vision of heads crowded around Patience's screen as they all pointed and argued. Patience came back on the line. 'Okay, sugar, I think we've got something.'

Patience relayed the information and said she was sending everything available in that direction now. Cops would converge from every direction but we were more than halfway there having started at West Kingsley so we were going to arrive first.

As I came off the phone, I turned to Sir Arthur and caught him grimacing. 'Sir Arthur, you are hurt.' I held up my hand to silence him when he tried to deflect me again. 'You are hurt. I'm going to take a look.' Once my seat belt was unclipped, I leaned across the center console and transmission tunnel and pulled his jacket open. Everything inside was sticky with blood. It looked bad. 'Does it hurt?'

'Tis a minor inconvenience, my dear. Think nothing of it,' he replied nonchalantly.

'I'm going to tear your shirt, okay, keep driving.' I grabbed the material were it was already cut and pulled it apart. It tore and he winced, the car jinking slightly but staying in its lane. He had been stabbed. It was low on his rib cage but there was no sound of escaping air and was too high to have caught any of his internal organs. Blood loss remained a concern.

Now I had even more reason to find Jennifer quickly; we had to end this before Sir Arthur passed out or bled to death.

Ten minutes later we were nearing the postcode Patience had given me. She said there should be a cottage nearby and a small parking place hidden behind the trees. The parking spot would be signposted though so should be easy to find.

We didn't find it.

We drove through the point the satnav on his phone said was the destination, went another mile, then doubled back and went slow. I could see the river through the trees, but there was no parking spot and no Jennifer's Volvo anywhere.

I was just about to call Patience again when something caught my eye. Light had glinted through the trees. 'Stop the car.' I shouted loud enough to startle my companion.

I patted his arm for comfort and stared through the trees. There was a car, I couldn't tell for sure if it was hers, but it was on the other side of the river. 'I think that's her,' I wailed. I felt crushed by the knowledge. We would never get to her in time. 'Any idea where the nearest bridge is?

'Miles away,' replied Sir Arthur.

'I'll have to try to swim it. The water is flowing east so I need you to back up a bit so I when I get washed downstream I end up somewhere near here. '

Sir Arthur drove off forward again. 'I think there was a junction just along here.'

'Um, I'm confused. What good is a junction?' I didn't want to go for a swim, the water would not be warm, and I didn't have a lot of body fat to protect me. I didn't feel like losing either so if I had to swim the river to catch the raving psycho then so be it.

To answer my question, Sir Arthur had a question of his own. 'Have you ever seen the James Bond Film, The Living Daylights?'

'Yeah, I guess? Is that the one with Timothy Dalton?'

Sir Arthur found the junction, went past it and then reversed into it and continued to reverse back while looking out of the back window. When he judged he had gone far enough, he stopped and turned to face me. 'Dalton made two movies as James Bond actually but the second was a big enough commercial failure for the studio to decide they needed to change everything including the actor. Anyway, they made a bunch of cars for the film and this is one of them.' He touched a button on the center console and a panel slid back to reveal an array of buttons.

'Holy crap,' I said as I stared at them. One was labeled laser, another missiles, yet another was machine guns.

Seeing my expression, he said. 'Oh, none of them work. Or, to be more accurate, none of them are armed. But there is one gadget that is functional. I had an engineer friend reinstall it and I have always wanted to try it out.'

'Oh, my lord! You're going to jump the river. Will we make it?'

Sir Arthur nodded his head and squared his jaw. 'No idea,' he replied, then stamped hard on the gas before I could say anything else. The Aston Martin Vantage's V8 engine propelled us toward the river at an insane speed. Ahead of us was a gap in the trees and a raised section of riverbank Sir Arthur would use as a natural ramp.

I was already too terrified for words, but I needed to shout that we were not going fast enough. There just wasn't enough road for us to build up the speed we needed. Then, from the corner of my eye, I saw him reach down to the console again. I tracked his hand to a button marked rocket engine.

I got to say, 'Oh, f...' but the rocket kicked in and I thought my eyeballs were going to touch the back of my skull as the car took off like... well, like a rocket. It hit the riverbank and blasted through it as much as over it. But the raised piece of land kicked the car upward and I caught a glimpse from my window of water beneath us.

We were in the air for no more than a second but that was enough to carry us to the other bank where the car ploughed through reeds and bushes as its momentum carried it onwards. Sir Arthur tried to steer but there was no chance he could control the car as it slid over the wet scrubland that bordered the river.

'I think the brakes are out,' he yelled as he fought for control and yanked on the hand brake. The car slewed around but finally stopped just short of the road on the other side of the river.

'Oh, my lord, we made it,' I breathed a massive sigh of relief. I was stunned and elated, but there was still a murder to stop. 'We have to get moving.'

Sir Arthur gave me a weary look. 'I think I might be done, my dear. Can you carry on without me? I am feeling a little woozy, truth be told.'

Thinking the worst but trying to keep it from my face and voice, I leaned across to his side of the car and checked his pulse. It was a little weak, but it was still banging away. The police were coming, I trusted that much, and there really wasn't anything I could do for him. So, I gripped his arm and said, 'You did a marvelous job, Sir Arthur. Marvelous. I am going to try to complete our quest now. I'll be back soon. You sit tight now, okay?'

'I shall rest awhile, m'lady and join you shortly,' he assured me. I doubted he would do anything other than pass out, but I intended to get this sewn up and get him to hospital before his condition worsened.

With a final pat on his arm, I slipped out of the door and closed it quietly. There was no way that Jennifer hadn't heard the racket we made, but until I found her and could see that the chief inspector was dead, I would continue to assume that he wasn't and could still be rescued.

Using Sir Arthur's phone, I tried Tempest's number again. I had it turned way down low and had my hand over the screen to shield the light coming from it. It rang and rang, but when it stopped ringing and a voice suddenly boomed in my ear, I almost dropped it.

'Tempest, it's Jane. I need you.' It was a simple statement, but I knew it would result in the reaction I required.

I could almost hear his breathing slow at the other end of the phone as he focused his attention and his voice was calm when he asked, 'What do you need me to do?'

'I'm out past Biddenden Lake, there's a killer here and she has Chief Inspector Quinn lined up as her next victim. I'm going to try to stop her,' I heard Tempest suck in a breath, and I knew he was about to try to talk me out of it, so I talked right over him. 'I'm doing it, okay. I don't know what's going to happen and I am terrified, but I have to try.'

'Terrified is good,' he said. 'Use that adrenalin to your advantage, control it and use it to make yourself faster or stronger. It will raise your pulse so watch out for feeling faint though.'

'There's an Aston Martin on the B1257 road that runs by the Tike river. There's an injured man in it and I owe him my life. Get him help, please. I have to go now.'

As I pulled the phone away from my ear, I heard Tempest say, 'Go with speed. I'll be there soon.' Then I left the phone because I had nowhere to put it, slipped out of the oversize jacket because it was cumbersome and set off toward where I thought I would find Jennifer.

Battle. Monday, December 5th 2149hrs

PICKING A FIGHT IS not really something I have ever done. I was one of the smaller kids in my class at school and, if I'm being honest, I was already a bit different back then. Some of the kids called me weird, but I just think they were afraid to see themselves reflected in me. They picked on me though and I rarely fought back.

Regardless of all that, I was on my way to find Jennifer and when I did, I was going to have to stop her from killing Quinn. I would have to fight her, and she was most likely armed still. I was not. Even if I was too late, and she had already drowned Quinn, I would still have to tackle her, the police were coming, and I could not let her get away.

Navigating by judgement and still not certain it was her car I saw on this side of the river, I stumbled across her almost immediately, coming around a tree by the lake's edge to find her manhandling CI Quinn out of the Volvo's boot.

She saw me just as I saw her and we both froze for a second. Then she giggled. 'I take it that was you making all that noise. It sounded like you crashed a car. Is Michelle dead?' I stared at her as my heart thumped in my chest. I couldn't see the knife but that didn't mean it wasn't there. 'I hope she is; she was becoming such a drag with all her rules.'

'She's with the police. It's over Jennifer.' Could I talk her into surrendering?

'She is the police, silly. If she's not dead, then she will explain how she was tracking down the crazy private investigator chick or something. You're the weirdo in this equation; no one is going to believe you. Anyway, I think I'll kill you now and then come back for this useless sack of meat.'

That's when the knife appeared in her right hand, glinting in the moonlight as she brandished it in front of her face. Then, coolly, she reached behind her back with her left hand and produced another knife to match the first.

'You want to be a girl, don't you? Maybe I can help with the operation.' She gave a little excited shiver of impending pleasure. 'Oooh, yeah. Maybe I'll keep your little thingy as a trophy.' She was done talking though, the smile dropping from her face as she held the knives to her sides and began to approach me.

I was petrified. Rooted to the spot and willing my feet to move. I felt like an animal at a slaughterhouse; waiting my turn to be butchered. Where the heck were the police? Involuntarily, I took a step back as she advanced, nearly losing my balance as my foot went into the lake.

She saw me stumble and ran at me, thrusting with the knife in her right hand and swinging at me with the left as I squealed and ducked away. Now we were both standing in the lake, ankle deep only but what if I could get her deeper? Could I stall her long enough for someone else to arrive if I just stayed out of her reach by wading out a bit? The woman can't swim; it was half of her lawyer's defense.

She came at me again with a growl, annoyed that I was managing to stay out of her reach. A wild swing I was easily able to dodge and another, forcing me back each time and I was knee deep now.

Then I ran out of luck as my legs fetched up against something. Momentum carried me further backwards and I pitched over, splashing down into the freezing cold water. All the air went out of my lungs as the frigid water hit my skin. I already believed I was cold; I hadn't been, but I was now.

A giggle brought my focus back as survival became the priority. Mercifully, my head remained above the water, though the back of my wig was now drenched and threatening to come off. Jennifer came at me, sensing that this was her chance.

My arms caught hold of the branch I tripped over and as she loomed over me, I yanked upward, snapping a piece off with both hands to parry her double downward stab. I was on my back in the water, with her face inches from mine. 'Why won't you just die?' she hissed in my face, then gave another little giggle.

She was on top of me and using her weight to push down the knives toward my face. She had the upper hand and all the advantage. In a movie, this would be the point when Sir Arthur, thought by the audience to be incapacitated, would appear for one last triumphant move to save the girl.

I waited a second with Jennifer's breath in my face, then accepted my fate and saved myself. Her crazy eyes were right in front of mine, If I wanted to, I could kiss her, she was that close.

Instead, I smiled at her. 'You forgot something, Jennifer.' When her brow crinkled in doubt, I said, 'I'm a guy and that makes me a lot stronger than you.' Then I stuck a foot in her gut and launched her high over my head and into the deep of the river beyond. Her surprised face quickly disappearing beneath the water with a splash.

Wondering if it was okay to laugh about the irony of her drowning, I let a small smirk flick across my face. Then I remembered how cold I was and dragged myself out of the mud and out of the river. The damned police still hadn't arrived. Then I heard the blissful sound of sirens in the distance and allowed myself a few seconds to rest on the riverbank, lying on my front and feeling spent.

The noise of the sirens grew louder and louder still. There was something wrong with it though. I lifted my head to check what I was hearing, but I didn't need to look to know what my brain was telling me; they were on the wrong side of the river. Just like Sir Arthur and I had, the satnav had directed them to an obvious spot but it was the wrong one.

Feeling frustrated, I put my hands under my body so I could get up. Maybe I could honk the horn on the Volvo and flash the lights to get their attention.

They would find us, plus I could turn the engine on and use the heaters to get some feeling back into my hands. Thinking that I really ought to check on the chief inspector as well, I levered myself unhappily back onto my elbows and turned my head so I could see where the police cars were.

Doing so saved my life.

'I learned to swim, freak!' Bedraggled and insane, Jennifer wasn't dead, she still had one of the knives, and she was throwing herself at me with it held in both hands. I rolled over, the knife digging into the grass where my head had been half a second earlier.

I got my hands and knees beneath me but not before she pulled the knife free. A sharp pain in my upper left arm told me her latest wild swing had hit home and I shrieked at the pain and shock of it.

Scrambling to get away, I slipped on the mud I myself had churned up, lost my forward momentum and crashed to the ground again.

She had me. And she knew it.

'You know what?' she gloated. 'I think I will cut it off and keep it. Just because you got me wet. Don't worry though. I'll do it after you're dead.'

Desperately searching for a weapon, any weapon, I found nothing, and on her knees, she moved in. I knew these were my last moments, so I clawed and kicked but she had the knife pointing toward me and was going to stick it in anything that came within stabbing distance. I felt it bite into my leg as I tried to kick her away, the pain barely registering over the level of panic I felt.

Then, above my head the blade flashed in the moonlight and a chunk of rock smashed into the side of Jennifer's head. The knife went flying, a small plop noise announcing its arrival in the river.

'You're under arrest,' said Chief Inspector Quinn. 'You do not have to say anything. But it may harm your defense if you do not mention when questioned something which you later rely on in court. Anything you do say may be given in evidence.' Jennifer was unconscious and hadn't heard one word of her rights, but that didn't seem to matter. 'You heard me read her rights, yes?'

I nodded weakly. 'Sure.'

'Good. That's the second time I've read her those rights for the same crime. I don't plan for there to be a third occurrence.' He looked across at me. 'Are you okay?'

I considered my answer to that question. I had a perfect opportunity to say something really cool, nothing came though, I was just too exhausted to think. I settled for, 'I'll live.'

The chief inspector looked out across the river and put his hands on his hips like Peter Pan. 'Good thing I was here to save the day then.' The back of my head was in the mud and it made a slight sucking noise as I lifted it to stare incredulously at the man. I felt a dire need to kick him, but I just didn't have the energy. He huffed out a breath, the cold air making it look like a cloud of steam. 'We need to get you into the warm. Hypothermia is a real risk at this time of year.' He grasped my right hand to pull me up, getting my arm around his shoulders so he could get me to the car.

There he found Jennifer's phone and dialed a number that put him through to an incident control center somewhere. Once he had identified himself, he said, 'I have apprehended the suspect. She is in my custody now and I have a casualty with me.' I managed to hold up a hand with two fingers extended. My teeth were chattering too badly for speech. 'Make that two casualties apparently. Yes, yes, I agree. A great day for Kent Police. What's that? Yes, I'm sure the chief constable will be very pleased. It's a team effort though. I cannot take all the credit.' The man was unbelievable, he was planning to claim the police had solved the case. He hadn't even thanked me for coming after him.

The car's engine was running, and warmth was beginning to bring life back to my arms and legs and face and everything else. When he finished the call, he helped me get my water-filled boots off and examined my cuts, declaring that none of them were life threatening, but most of them would leave scars. He continually ducked his head back out of the car to check on Jennifer but she hadn't moved at any point.

I put my head back and waited for the belated cavalry to arrive.

Mopping Up. Monday, December 5th 2254hrs

THE WAIL OF APPROACHING sirens finally cut off when they arrived ten minutes later, police by the truckload descending on the little riverbank as more and more cars appeared.

I was warm enough now to be able to speak so I swiveled around in my seat and pushed the door open, a move I regretted the instant the cold air outside hit my skin and wet clothes. I had rested long enough though, Sir Arthur needed medical attention and they might ignore his car if I didn't point him out.

'Wait, miss,' insisted a short male police officer as I left the car and began to gingerly step barefoot across the gravel. 'We need to get you some help, I think. An ambulance will be here any moment.'

'I have to check on my friend. He's parked just along the road.'

'Is that the big chap in James Bond's car?' he asked. Seeing me nod, he smiled, 'We found him already, dispatch got a call to look out for him. He's going to be okay, I think, though he was delirious, spouting some fanciful tale about jumping the river in his car.'

Relief washed through me as the man was joined by several of his colleagues. 'We need to get you out of those wet clothes, miss,' said one. 'I'll fetch some blankets from the squad car.' Then sensing he had just insisted the petite blonde woman take her clothes off for the male audience, he called over two female officers to assist me.

As I shivered in the cold, one of them started to help me by unzipping my dress at the back. 'Good thing Chief Inspector Quinn was here to rescue you,' she commented as her colleague slipped an oversize police jacket around my shoulders. With the jacket in place, I peeled off my dress, doing my best to keep as little skin exposed to the cold as possible.

I wanted to tell them that the chief inspector hadn't rescued me, but of course, he had. Right at the end, his efforts had saved the day. How much credit I would get was yet to be seen, though I suspected it would be very little. I wasn't even getting paid.

Above the background noise of engines and chatter by the riverbank, the sound of a tuned German engine announced that Tempest was about to arrive. The sound cut out a hundred metres short, doubtless stopped by a police officer as they temporarily closed the road to deal with the incident.

He found his way through on foot a few minutes later, spotting me easily as I rested in the back of a warm police car. 'Hi, Jane,' he waved through the car's window.

Slowly, because my limbs felt heavy and sluggish, I opened the door. Cold air flooded in. 'Hi, Tempest. I closed the case.'

'So, I heard. Are you okay?'

'Sure,' I answered with a shrug. 'Mostly I am cold and tired.' I didn't mention the cuts and bruises, they would heal soon enough.

He nodded his understanding. 'It's a bit cold out here, shuffle over and I'll get in.' I did that, making room for him to get in and close the door so the warmth could return. 'I feel like I have missed something.' Tempest was hanging his head guiltily as if he believed my situation this evening was due to an omission on his part. 'You could have been hurt or killed,' he added with an angry huff at himself.

'It's okay, Tempest. None of those things happened. I accidentally triggered the attack when I got involved. Jennifer's accomplice is a police officer, she knew about me from the very first visit to the police station. She's the one that tried to kill me by setting fire to Karen Gilbert's house. I thought it was the Sandman, but it was her.' I spent the next ten minutes telling him about waking up in their lock-up and the ride in the car and being rescued by Sir Arthur.

'I knew there was something about him,' laughed Tempest when I got to that bit. 'What a crazy old man. I wonder if he will give up the ogre thing now.'

I doubted it, but who could tell. I finished the story with my fight with Jennifer and the chief inspector's last moment save.

Tempest said, 'I want you to take a couple of days. Come back when you are ready. I am going to speak with the police, make sure they have everything they need from you for now. They will want a statement I expect.'

'Yes, they did say that.' With nothing left to say and the flashing lights of an ambulance now making its way through the police cordon, Tempest opened the door and went to do Tempest things.

The ambulance appeared as yet more cops showed up, the paramedics' first task was to deal with the still unconscious Jennifer. The blow to her head had split the skin on her scalp but once they had assessed that her condition wasn't life-threatening, one of them quickly turned his attention to me. Still sitting in the back of the police car, he checked me over and assessed me. I had three nasty cuts, one to my left arm where the blade had cut down to my tricep muscle and two on my right leg from my failed attempts to kick her away. Apart from bruises and a dance with hypothermia, I was going to be fine, he assured me. Instant gluey stitch things went on the cuts to close them and I was packed into an ambulance where it was warm and dry. Sir Arthur was already in there.

'Lady Jane!' he hallooed me raucously. 'I understand you were victorious in your quest. Well, done, dear lady.'

'Thank you, Sir Arthur.' I patted his hand across the center divide of the ambulance. 'I could not have done it without your help.'

'Nonsense, dear girl. You would have found a way to overcome, I'm sure.'

'I would have been killed by Michelle at the river,' I argued. 'You rescued me there and then got me here. How could I have arrived here without you? I don't even own a car.'

Instantly he replied, 'Then I must insist you take the Aston.'

I thought for a moment that he was joking. He wasn't of course, but I couldn't accept it. So, as the ambulance pulled away from the spot by the river, we took to arguing about my need for a worthy steed to carry me on future quests.

I kept saying no and coming up with reasons why I couldn't take his car, even though he had many more cars in his garage. In the end, from fatigue as much as anything, I gave in.

'Wonderful!' he exclaimed, sounding overcome with joy at the prospect of giving up his toy. 'I shall have it repaired and valeted and delivered to your place of work.' Satisfied, he settled his head back onto the raised portion of his stretcher and fell promptly asleep.

The paramedic in the back with us, who had until then been quietly monitoring Sir Arthur's drip and both out vitals, said, 'What was all that about? Was he trying to give you a car?'

'Yes. An Aston Martin. It's too much though. It's fancier even than my boss's car.'

'What does your boss drive?' she asked as she made a note on a tablet.

'A gorgeous red Porsche.' The woman was just making idle chitchat to keep my mind off my injuries, but she looked up sharply when I described Tempest's car.

'You work for Tempest Michaels. Don't you? I thought you looked familiar. I'm Alice, Jagjit's wife. I was just with Tempest in France.'

'Oh, my word.' The funny coincidence gave us something to chat about for the next few minutes as the ambulance swept through the quiet nighttime countryside on its way to Maidstone Hospital. I was tired and sore and the last few days had been some of the weirdest in my life. Yet I was also exhilarated by the adventure and I knew that I no longer had any option: I was going to be an investigator from now on.

Epilogue

TWO DAYS LATER LIFE was getting back to normal. Tempest had told me I could stay off work if I needed to and should return when I felt ready. I craved the routine of going to work though, I wanted something to do. So, after convalescing for Tuesday and Wednesday to make sure I was over the minor case of hyperthermia, I made my way to work.

I had to take the bus, which was fine; it stopped just along the road from Gran's house and delivered me to Rochester High Street. I was going to need to buy a car soon though. Despite Sir Arthur's promise to give me his car, I doubted he meant it, but I could take Tempest up on his offer of an interest-free loan and buy myself something sensible.

Because I took the bus, I approached the office from the front instead of the back for the first time ever. The lights were on but I was later arriving than usual, again because of the bus, so Tempest and Amanda were already in.

Neither was visible though when I pushed through the front door to the warm space inside. There was still a faintly detectable odour of fishiness though I questioned if I could detect it only because I knew it was there.

'Hello?' I called out. Both their office doors were open, but the office itself was eerily quiet. I unwound my scarf and hung it on the coat stand as I moved through the office space, passing the couches arranged for visitors and onwards to the offices at the back. Glancing inside, I could see they were indeed not there, but I could see movement outside in the darkness of the carpark.

I pushed open the door that led to the corridor to the back door. Just then, the back door opened and my colleagues came through it, talking animatedly in excited tones.

When they saw me, Amanda said, 'There she is. You lucky girl.'

'Hi guys. What's going on?' I asked.

Tempest smiled a wide smile and held up his right hand, from which he then released a car key and fob so it dangled. 'That's quite the car you have out there. Sorry, we couldn't resist going for a look.'

Seeing my confused face, Amanda said, 'Didn't you know it was coming? A man dropped it off a few minutes ago.'

'It's a gift from Sir Arthur apparently. The man said you would know what that meant,' added Tempest.

He handed me the key and I found my hands were shaking when I took it. The fob bore an Aston Martin insignia. Letting my feet drag me onward to the backdoor, I pushed it open, and there before me was the dark grey, sleek, expensive car. Tempest and Amanda followed me back out.

Standing next to me as I stared at it, Tempest asked, 'What do you think?'

I gulped. 'It's beautiful.' The others nodded at my murmured comment. 'There's a few things about it that you don't know though.' In response to their raised eyebrows, I opened the car and proceeded to show them the switches and buttons hidden inside the panels of the cab. When I hit the button marked machine guns, two panels slid open on the bonnet and two machine guns sprang into view.'

'Whoa!' Amanda's surprise was shared with Tempest who whistled appreciatively.

From outside in the dark, I could see into the light office right in front of the parked cars, so I saw the front door open and knew it was time to stop marveling at my new toy. My brain was telling me I couldn't accept such a gift, but my heart certainly wanted to and I doubted Sir Arthur would take no for an answer.

The person coming through the front door was the postman, coming in rather than pushing his delivery through the letter box because he had a parcel as well. He was on his way back out the door as we arrived back in the warm office. He shot us all a wave and was gone.

Tempest and Amanda filtered into their offices to get on with whatever work they had and I went to my desk. The parcel was a box about nine inches square and wrapped in brown paper. It was addressed to me.

I tore it open with my nails and lifted the lid to find an old vinyl record inside. As I reached in for it, I realised I had never held one before. It was a single; a record containing one song and not an album, I knew that much from watching TV but as I picked it up to inspect it, my blood froze.

The record had a paper cover with a hole in the middle to reveal the center of the record itself. There I found the title: Mr Sandman by the Chordettes.

Feeling the world spin beneath my feet, I put a hand out to steady myself, leaning forward to dip my head as a case of the whirlies gripped me. With a gasp for air, I opened my eyes and spotted writing on the base of the box. The record had obscured it but now I could see what was written: I'm going to sing you to sleep.

The End

What's next for the Blue Moon gang?

EVERY SECOND GENERATION OF the Hale line dies at the hands of an un-nameable monster on his 80th birthday. The current Lord Hale turns 80 this Saturday.

To protect himself, Lord Hale has invited paranormal investigation experts Tempest Michaels and Amanda Harper plus their friends and a whole host of other guests from different fields of supernatural exploration for a birthday dinner at his mansion.

As they sit down for dinner, the lights start to dim and a moaning noise disturbs the polite conversation. Has Lord Hale placed his faith in the right people, or just led them to share his doom?

Finding themselves trapped, Tempest and Amanda, with friends Big Ben and Patience must join forces with a wizard, some scientists, and occult experts, ghost chasers, witches, and other assorted idiots as they fight to make it through the night in one piece.

Could this be their final adventure? Will Tempest finally be proven wrong about the paranormal?

LORD HALE'S
MONSTER

BLUE MOON INVESTIGATIONS BOOK THIRTEEN

STEVE HIGGS

More Books By Steve Higgs

Blue Moon Investigations
Paranormal Nonsense
The Phantom of Barker Mill
Amanda Harper Paranormal Detective
The Klowns of Kent
Dead Pirates of Cawsand
In the Doodoo With Voodoo
The Witches of East Malling
Crop Circles, Cows and Crazy Aliens
Whispers in the Rigging
Bloodlust Blonde – a short story
Paws of the Yeti
Under a Blue Moon – A Paranormal
Detective Origin Story
Night Work
Lord Hale's Monster
The Herne Bay Howlers
Undead Incorporated
The Ghoul of Christmas Past
The Sandman
Jailhouse Golem
Shadow in the Mine
Ghost Writer

Felicity Philips Investigates
To Love and to Perish
Tying the Noose
Aisle Kill Him
A Dress to Die For
Wedding Ceremony Woes

Patricia Fisher Cruise Mysteries
The Missing Sapphire of Zangrabar
The Kidnapped Bride
The Director's Cut
The Couple in Cabin 2124
Doctor Death
Murder on the Dancefloor
Mission for the Maharaja
A Sleuth and her Dachshund in Athens
The Maltese Parrot
No Place Like Home

Patricia Fisher Mystery Adventures
What Sam Knew
Solstice Goat
Recipe for Murder
A Banshee and a Bookshop
Diamonds, Dinner Jackets, and Death
Frozen Vengeance
Mug Shot
The Godmother
Murder is an Artform
Wonderful Weddings and Deadly
Divorces
Dangerous Creatures

Patricia Fisher: Ship's Detective Series
The Ship's Detective
Fitness Can Kill
Death by Pirates
First Dig Two Graves

Albert Smith Culinary Capers
Pork Pie Pandemonium
Bakewell Tart Bludgeoning
Stilton Slaughter
Bedfordshire Clanger Calamity
Death of a Yorkshire Pudding
Cumberland Sausage Shocker
Arbroath Smokie Slaying
Dundee Cake Dispatch
Lancashire Hotpot Peril
Blackpool Rock Bloodshed
Kent Coast Oyster Obliteration
Eton Mess Massacre
Cornish Pasty Conspiracy

Realm of False Gods
Untethered magic
Unleashed Magic
Early Shift
Damaged but Powerful
Demon Bound
Familiar Territory
The Armour of God
Live and Die by Magic
Terrible Secrets

About the Author

At school, the author was mostly disinterested in every subject except creative writing, for which, at age ten, he won his first award. However, calling it his first award suggests that there have been more, which there have not. Accolades may come but, in the meantime, he is having a ball writing mystery stories and crime thrillers and claims to have more than a hundred books forming an unruly queue in his head as they clamour to get out. He lives in the south-east corner of England with a duo of lazy sausage dogs. Surrounded by rolling hills, brooding castles, and vineyards, he doubts he will ever leave, the beer is just too good.

If you are a social media fan, you should copy the link below into your browser to join my very active Facebook group. You'll find a host of friends waiting there, some of whom have been with me from the very start.

My Facebook group get first notification when I publish anything new, plus cover reveals and free short stories, but more than that, they all interact with each other, sharing inside jokes, and answering question.

f facebook.com/stevehiggsauthor

You can also keep updated with my books via my website:

https://stevehiggsbooks.com/

Printed in Great Britain
by Amazon

36561330R00111